THE RETURN OF THE OTHER MRS. WATSON

A new collection of puzzlers featuring the second wife of Dr. John H. Watson, of Sherlock Holmes fame. This time Amelia is plunged into a series of affairs that include the case of a carriage that vanishes into thin air, a jewellery theft on board an ocean liner, and an ancient royal document that may challenge the state of the sovereignty itself. As Amelia solves each case with resourcefulness and wit, she demonstrates the Holmesian adage: 'Once you eliminate the impossible, whatever remains, no matter how improbable, must be the truth.'

Books by Michael Mallory
in the Linford Mystery Library:

THE OTHER MRS. WATSON

MICHAEL MALLORY

THE RETURN OF THE OTHER MRS. WATSON

Complete and Unabridged

LINFORD
Leicester

First published in Great Britain

First Linford Edition
published 2016

A catalogue record for this book is available
from the British Library.

ISBN 978–1–4448–3059–0

Published by
F. A. Thorpe (Publishing)
Anstey, Leicestershire

Set by Words & Graphics Ltd.
Anstey, Leicestershire
Printed and bound in Great Britain by
T. J. International Ltd., Padstow, Cornwall

This book is printed on acid-free paper

Contents

Contents

The Adventure of
the Illustrious Patient

A loud, jarring ring shattered the quiet of my home, and it was several seconds before I was able to identify the horrid noise as the new telephone that my husband insisted we needed, one whose sound was far louder and more grating than any I had yet encountered.

Uncradling the listening mechanism, I held it to my ear and said, 'Yes, hello, what is it?' into the mouthpiece.

'Mrs. Watson,' said a voice I recognized only too well.

'Mr. Holmes, I do not wish to speak to you,' I said firmly.

'I beg your pardon?'

'You should be begging my forgiveness as well.'

'Mrs. Watson, I believe you are mistaking — '

'I am mistaking nothing, least of all

that hole I found in John's hat after he returned from your latest escapade. A bullet hole, Mr. Holmes, and had it struck one inch lower I would be wearing mourning colours and more than likely find you opposing me in court for the widow's jointure!'

'Mrs. Watson, please — '

'No, Mr. Holmes, I have remained silent far too long. I have managed to put up with your domination of my husband for his sake, but I will not endure it one day longer! You had John during his youth, but I have him now, and I am not going to sit back and watch him slaughtered in the late summer of his life as a result of your foolish police games. I will forbid him to ever see you again if that is what it takes to reclaim him. Therefore, Mr. Holmes, I bid you goodbye.'

'Please do not disconnect,' the voice entreated. 'A pretty tirade, madam. I only hope to be present should you decide to reprise it for Sherlock's benefit.'

'But . . . is this not Sherlock Holmes?'

'No, I am Mycroft Holmes, Sherlock's elder brother.'

Dear God in Heaven, there were two of them? 'I must apologise, Mr. Holmes,' I stammered in embarrassment, 'but you sound very much like your brother.'

'So I have been told. Now then, is the good doctor about?'

'No, he is still at his surgery. Would you like the address?'

'I have the address, thank you, but the matter in which I require his consultation is rather delicate, requiring far greater privacy than a public surgery could offer. When do you expect him home?'

'He usually returns by six o'clock.'

'Expect us at six o'clock, then,' said Mycroft Holmes. 'Oh, and please be so good as to send your young maid Missy away before we get there.' The telephone connection broke off.

Us, he had said. Obviously I was to be treated to both Mycroft and Sherlock Holmes (*Mycroft* and *Sherlock* — what could their parents have been thinking?) bringing to our doorstep some business so dire that our maid could not be party to it.

I thought of ringing John at his surgery

to warn him of our impending Holmes invasion, but decided against it. Instead, I informed Missy of her unexpected evening out, news that she accepted a trifle more cheerfully than decorum warranted, I thought. But only after she had gone did a faintly disturbing thought enter my head: I had never before spoken to Mycroft Holmes, never before known of his existence, in fact.

So how was it that he knew we employed a young maid named Missy?

I was still puzzling over this when the knock came at our door, precisely at the stroke of six. Since John had not yet arrived home, I prepared as best I could to handle our visitors alone. Upon opening the door, I saw a portly, bearded gentleman of roughly sixty, clad in a dark suit and greatcoat and wearing a black slouch hat. While I could detect no resemblance to Sherlock Holmes in the broad, pleasant face, there was something faintly familiar about the man, who regarded me with sparkling blue eyes.

'Mr. Holmes, how nice to meet you,' I said, offering my hand. At first he seemed uncertain what to do with it, but then smiled and took it in his.

'Do come in,' I said, 'and let me apologise once more for my earlier outburst.'

'Outburst?' he responded, in a voice clearly different from the one I had heard on the telephone. Just then another man appeared behind him, one whose enormous frame nearly blocked out all of the light from the hall.

'How do you do, Mrs. Watson,' the second man said, 'I am Mycroft Holmes.' The elder Holmes was easily as tall as his brother, if not taller, though as corpulent as the detective was emaciated. The poor man was panting and sweating profusely, no doubt the result of having forced his bulk up the stairs.

Leading them into the sitting room (our home, unfortunately, does not have a proper drawing room), I bid them be seated.

'I prefer standing,' replied the man with the beard, giving each 'r' sound a Teutonic roll.

'I must, therefore, stand also,' Mycroft

Holmes said, rather unhappily. Refusing refreshments, both men remained silent until the sound of the front door opening captured their attention. 'Ah, that must be the redoubtable Dr. Watson,' Mycroft said, pulling an old repeater watch from his pocket, and adding: 'Four minutes late.'

Excusing myself, I stepped out to the door and greeted John with a light kiss on the cheek.

'We have visitors, dear,' I said.

'Oh?' he said, removing his coat and hat and hanging them on the coat rack. 'Who?'

'One is Mycroft Holmes, and the other — '

'Mycroft Holmes! Great Scott, what is he doing here?'

Mr. Holmes then lumbered into view. 'I am sure it must be something of a shock, Doctor, to find me out of my natural habitat, the Diogenes Club, but I come on a matter of great importance. There is someone I want you to meet.'

We hastened into the sitting room, but as soon as John clapped eyes on the

6

bearded man he froze in place, his jaw dropping. 'Your Majesty,' he muttered.

'His what?' I cried.

'May I introduce His Royal Majesty King Edward the Seventh,' Mycroft Holmes said, and the bearded man nodded curtly.

'Your M-majesty,' I stammered, curtseying rather awkwardly, 'please forgive me for not recognizing you.'

The King smiled. 'That is a tribute to our Mr. Holmes here,' he said. 'It is he who has taught me how to dress and act unlike a King for those times when I wish to leave the palace.'

'With Your Majesty's permission,' I said, 'I should like to sit down before I faint.'

He nodded again and I sank onto the sofa. John, however, remained standing. 'This is, indeed, quite a singular honour,' he said. 'How may we be of service to Your Majesty?'

'His Majesty is in dire need of medical attention,' Mycroft answered.

'Surely there is the Royal Physician.'

'For a variety of reasons, we cannot

take Sir Francis into our confidence regarding this matter.'

Pulling a cigar from his inner breast pocket, the King bit off the tip and lit it from a match suddenly proffered by Mycroft Holmes. 'Doctor Watson,' he began, 'were you aware of the fact that I nearly died of illness in my thirtieth year?'

'No, sir, I was not,' John replied.

'Too true. Then, two years ago, shortly before my coronation, I was stricken with appendicitis which necessitated emergency surgery.'

'Thank heavens Your Majesty received prompt attention.'

'Indeed,' said Mycroft Holmes, 'but the point we are striving to make, Doctor, is that His Majesty had never enjoyed more public and Parliamentary support as doing those two periods of illness. His Majesty's appendix, in fact, deserves a great deal of credit for pulling this nation from the threat of European isolation, which lingering resentment over the Boer War had cast over us.'

'Great Scott,' John muttered.

His Majesty blew out a billow of royal

smoke. 'It is a good idea for kings to be ill from time to time,' he said. 'That is why I want you to make me so.'

John glanced over at Mycroft, as though asking for a translation. 'Make you ill, Your Majesty?'

'As you probably know,' Mycroft replied, 'His Majesty has recently returned from Paris, which was the final step in forging a pact with France and, we hope, Russia.'

'Nicky is a good boy, he will agree,' the King stated, and upon reflection I realized he was speaking of Tsar Nicholas, one of his many regal relatives.

Obviously uncomfortable from the prolonged period of standing, Mycroft Holmes eased his bulk against the edge of John's writing bureau (which creaked dangerously) and continued: 'The goal of this pact is nothing short of ensuring peace in Europe through alliances that will reduce the power and influence of some of our more bellicose neighbours.'

'Like Germany,' I blurted out, then immediately regretted it, remembering that another of the King's nephews ruled that empire.

But Mycroft Holmes only smiled. 'I see you follow world affairs, Mrs. Watson, how admirable.' I smiled back, thankful that he had not automatically added *for a woman*, as his brother would no doubt have said. He went on: 'Finalizing such a wide-reaching intercontinental accord is a highly delicate matter, and one that requires unquestioning support — the kind that His Majesty feels he could rely upon only if he were suddenly taken seriously ill.

'At present, however, His Majesty has the misfortune of being, to use the vernacular, healthy as a stallion. Therefore, Doctor Watson, we require a drug of some sort that will give His Majesty every symptom of serious illness, be convincing enough to fool the Royal Physician, yet leave no lasting effects. And time is, I am afraid, of the essence. His Majesty is scheduled to make an appearance at a state dinner at the palace on Friday, to which you are both invited, though he will be forced to cancel the appearance because of the illness that you, Doctor, will provide him with.'

Dinner at Buckingham Palace! My heart leapt at the news! But Friday was the day after tomorrow.

'I have nothing to wear to the Palace,' I blurted out.

Mycroft Holmes smiled once more. 'I shall instruct one of the court dressmakers to contact you,' he said. 'A carriage will come to pick you up on Friday at eight o'clock sharp, so please be ready. The fate of Europe is in your hands, Doctor Watson. Do not let us down.' Then, turning to the King, he added, 'I believe our task is finished here, Your Majesty.'

As we bowed to the sovereign, Mr. Holmes lumbered to the door, opened it, and looked out to see if anyone else was present. Satisfied, he motioned for the King to follow him.

My head was absolutely spinning from this unexpected visit. 'I did not realize, darling, that you had friends in such high places.'

'Frankly, neither did I,' John replied. 'Oh, I knew that Mycroft worked for the government, and Holmes once remarked

11

that at times he thought his brother *was* the government, but I never took the comment seriously. Well, my dear, if I am commanded to make the King ill, I had better get to it.'

John spent the rest of the evening poring over medical books and dictionaries, stopping only for strong coffee or to refill his pipe. He was still at it when Missy arrived back from her unexpected evening out, and even as I finally went to bed some time after midnight, taking a book with me (and while Mr. Dickens remains one of the loves of my life, he is an altogether poor substitute for my husband in bed). I read until my eyes could no longer focus on the words, at which point I set aside my book and extinguished the light, hoping John would soon join me.

The next thing I knew, however, the morning light was creeping through the bedroom curtains. I reached for John, finding only cold, empty sheets.

Pulling my warm robe around me, I made my way to the sitting room where I found a note in John's hand on the table, informing me that he had already dressed and gone out, hoping an early-morning walk would clear his mind.

Midway through my lonely breakfast the wretched telephone jangled again, startling Missy so badly that the poor girl nearly dropped her tray. Once again it was Mycroft Holmes on the line, this time ringing to tell me when to expect the dress fitters.

My excitement steadily rose until some hours later when a prim woman and her young assistant arrived, laden with materials of all kinds and colours. I selected a stylish dark green velvet and was assured that, incredibly, the gown would be ready on the morrow.

The rest of the day passed uneventfully until John arrived home from his surgery, so thoroughly exhausted that he was barely able to stay awake through dinner.

'Really, darling, you must get some sleep,' I said as I poured him an after-dinner whisky.

'I intend to,' he yawned, 'because I believe I have finally found the answer. I pray so, anyway. It is so simple, I spent an entire day overlooking it.'

True to his word, the poor dear slept that night like a hibernating bear, though I tossed and turned, far too excited to sleep. What was the Palace like? I wondered. And what other dignitaries and nobles would be at the dinner?

At some point, though, I dropped off into a deep, dreamless slumber, from which I was awakened very late the next morning by Missy after John had already left for the day. My beautiful new evening gown was delivered shortly before tea-time, and by the time John returned home I was already coiffed and bejewel-led for the evening's festivities.

At precisely the appointed time, a coach appeared at the curb, and we enjoyed a peaceful ride through the city to Buckingham Palace. Although looking elegantly handsome as always in his evening clothes, John seemed lost in a dark, troubled cloud of thought.

I felt my excitement returning fourfold as we entered the palace gardens and passed through stately iron gates which opened upon the eastern forecourt, where a queue of like vehicles slowly progressed up the carriage drive.

Our coach, however, did not follow the others, but suddenly veered around them and took us to a private door at the grounds side of the palace, where the unmistakable form of Mycroft Holmes was waiting.

'Come this way, please,' he said as we stepped down from the coach, John helping me down with one hand while clutching his medical bag with the other.

I heard the sounds of a spirited gathering coming from somewhere inside the palace as John and I followed Mycroft up a back staircase and down a hallway, finally coming to a closed door. Giving a quick, rhythmic rap, Mycroft awaited the reply then led us in. To our utter shock, we found ourselves in the King's private bedroom!

Save for the crossed swords and crest that were affixed rather melodramatically to one wall, the room was tastefully and simply decorated in a white and gold motif. In the centre of the room the King, now in official raiment, was holding court over a small group of people.

15

Standing just behind His Majesty was a handsome young officer whom Mycroft introduced to us as Lieutenant Benjamin Breakstone, the King's equerry. Next we were introduced to Lord Landsdowne, the Foreign Secretary, and a man who carried himself with great portentousness, as though he was posing for an official portrait at all times.

The only other woman, aside from myself, was a coquettish young thing whose dimpled smile was perpetually fixed upon His Majesty, who frequently returned the attention. 'May I present Mademoiselle Perrault, whom His Majesty met on his recent trip to Paris,' Mycroft said. He needed to say no more, since I recalled the tales I had heard during my days in the theatre regarding the then-Prince of Wales' devotion to beautiful women, most notably the actress Mrs. Langtry. Obviously, his coronation had done as little to rein in this behaviour in His Majesty as had his marriage.

There was another figure in the room; a tall, thin man whose back was turned to us in order to examine a large oil portrait hanging on the far wall. When the man faced us, my heart sank.

'Of course you know my brother, Sherlock,' said Mycroft Holmes as the detective bowed to us.

'I did not realize Mr. Holmes was party to this little deception,' I said, striving to maintain civility.

'Oh, yes; it was Sherlock who suggested that we turn to your husband, he not having the proper medical knowledge himself,' Mycroft answered.

I was about to challenge that statement, knowing of Mr. Holmes's obsession with poisons, as well as just about any other manner of death and destruction, when Mademoiselle Perrault suddenly lunged for the King, brazenly touching his arm and shoulder with satin-gloved hands.

'Must you go through with this, Your Majesty?' she cooed. 'It sounds so dangerous.' In her accent, the last word came out *don-joor-aus*.

'I have been told I may trust Doctor Watson completely,' the King replied. 'Shall we be about it, then?'

'Very well, Your Majesty,' John replied crisply, and for the first time I saw in my husband a vestige of the former soldier, a man trained to carry out his orders.

He opened his bag and took out a small vial of liquid. 'This is a solution distilled from tincture of ipecac, which is normally used to induce regurgitation for someone who has swallowed poison.'

'Will this solution in any way harm His Majesty?' Lieutenant Breakstone snapped.

'If too much were to be given, yes,' John replied, withdrawing a needle from his bag, 'but in the correct dosage, it will simply make His Majesty sick, as he requested.'

'For your sake, sir, you had better be right,' the equerry said fiercely.

Ignoring the implied threat from Lieutenant Breakstone, John went about drawing up a small amount of the solution into the needle, then offered the vial to Mycroft. 'Please take this and do what you will with it,' he said, then placed the needle on a small silver tray, set it down on an antique French table, then faced the King.

'By preparing this solution, Your Majesty, I have done as you commanded.

However, at no time was I instructed to actually administer the dose. Therefore, in light of the oath I took as a medical man and the regard in which I hold the Crown, I respectfully refuse to do so unless so ordered by your gracious self.'

The King's eyebrows shot up at this and he looked to Mycroft Holmes, whose face bore an inscrutable expression. I prayed that in following his conscience, John had not overstepped his bounds!

The terrible silence that followed was shattered by Sherlock Holmes. 'With Your Majesty's permission, I will administer the dose in place of my friend.'

'You, Mr. Holmes?' the equerry said sceptically.

'Oh, don't worry, he has ample experience with needles,' I said, only to receive an elbow nudge from my husband.

Carefully picking the tray, Sherlock Holmes examined the needle, then bid His Majesty to roll up his sleeve. But even as this was taking place, a loud *bang!* was heard just outside the door to the King's chambers.

'Good Lord! That sounded like a

gunshot!' Lord Landsdowne exclaimed.

'Everyone stay here,' Sherlock Holmes ordered, setting down the needle and dashing to the door. The confusion that followed lasted only a brief minute before Holmes returned, carefully holding out the remnants of an exploded firecracker.

The King sighed. 'My grandson David's work, no doubt. He rather enjoys creating a commotion. Carry on, Mr. Holmes.'

As the rest of us looked on (save for Mademoiselle Perrault, who turned away), Mr. Holmes injected the solution into the arm of the King, who did not so much as wince, then placed the needle back on the tray.

'How quickly will the symptoms emerge, doctor?' Mycroft asked.

'Nausea will occur very quickly,' John responded, 'followed by fatigue and light-headedness.'

'My brother and I will stay with His Majesty until the first signs of sickness occur, then send for the Royal Physician — for show, you understand. The rest of you, go downstairs and enjoy the dinner. Lord Landsdowne, would you be so good as to lead our guests to the ballroom?'

It was Lieutenant Breakstone, however, who took command, marching us through a series of magnificent hallways, while Lord Landsdowne engaged Mademoiselle Perrault in conversation, frequently in French. Before long, we arrived at the ornately-crafted Grand Staircase, and continued on a path that eventually led us to the chandelier-filled ballroom.

We took our seats at the lavishly-set banquet table and chatted amiably with our fellow diners through the first course, which consisted of an excellent turtle soup. Halfway through the pheasant, however, I noticed John's gaze suddenly focus on a man rushing towards the table. 'Good heavens, that is Lacking,' he said.

'I am hard pressed to find anything lacking, darling,' I responded.

'No, Sir Francis Lacking, the Royal Physician; and judging from his expression, something has gone wrong.'

I felt myself go cold as he spoke those words, and watched as Sir Francis rushed to the chair occupied by Lord Landsdowne and demanded that he come with him. This likewise attracted the attention of the King's equerry and Mademoiselle Perrault (whose very presence at the table I felt to be a brazen slap in the face of the Queen). Those two quickly rose and went with Holmes and Sir Francis, and after a quick flurry of pardons to those sitting nearest us, John and I followed.

We arrived en masse to the King's bedroom, each of us, I think, shocked at what we saw.

The King was lying motionless in the large canopy bed, his robust countenance now pale and waxen, his eyes open but vacant, and his breathing so shallow as to go unnoticed.

'Dear heavens,' I exclaimed, 'is he — '

'His Majesty is still alive,' said Sir Francis, 'though for how much longer I cannot say. Mr. Holmes has already informed me of this foolish scheme.' He then turned to John.

'You, sir, what in God's name could you have been thinking to agree to such an abominable plan? And what did you inject into His Majesty?'

'It was ipecac,' John answered, 'and I

assure you, sir, that the dosage I prescribed would not harm His Majesty. Surely you must realize, Sir Francis, that even an overdose of ipecac would cause convulsions, not lethargy. May I please examine His Majesty myself?'

'No, sir, you have done quite enough,' Sir Francis replied icily.

Suddenly frightened for my husband, I turned to Mycroft Holmes. 'Please, Mr. Holmes, do something, say something.'

'It is out of my hands now, Mrs. Watson,' he replied, casually. 'I am sorry.'

'Out of your hands?' I shouted. 'May I remind you, sir, that you were the instigator of this little charade!'

'Mrs. Watson, pray control yourself,' broke in the calm, steady voice of Sherlock Holmes. 'I ask everyone to refrain from jumping to conclusions. Remember, it was I who administered the dose, not Doctor Watson. Furthermore, he is quite right in stating that the toxin he distilled for injection would not cause the symptoms you see before you, which leads us to only one conclusion: that the King has been injected with another kind of toxin.'

'That's impossible, Holmes!' John cried. 'I filled the needle myself!'

'True. But if you recall, just as I was preparing to inject His Majesty, a firecracker exploded in the hall. I returned the needle to its tray and went out to investigate. In the confusion that followed, it would have been easy for anyone in this room to tamper with the needle, replacing the innocuous solution with a deadly one.'

'Sir, are you accusing one of us?' bristled Lord Landsdowne.

'I am, my lord; and furthermore, I have taken steps that will clearly reveal the guilty party.' After this pronouncement, the room fell silent as a tomb. Holmes went on: 'Immediately after I relieved Watson of the needle, I took the liberty of coating it with a special chemical that reacts with the natural oils found on the human skin.' He then raised his hand for all to see. There were traces of bright orange on his fingers. 'Anyone else who touched it will likewise be marked. I would like to examine the hands of everyone in this room.'

Mycroft was the first to present his

hands, followed by John, then myself (though I could hardly be considered a suspect). Lieutenant Breakstone presented his hands in a strange kind of snapping salute, first showing his palms, then the backs, and then the palms again. After a fair amount of grumbling, Lord Landsdowne offered his hands for view, as did a petulant Mademoiselle Perrault. The last to follow suit was Sir Francis Lacking, who appeared highly insulted at the very request. No one's hands bore any trace of chemical staining.

'Rather blows your theory out of the water, Holmes,' Lord Landsdowne said, somewhat nervously. But then I remembered something.

'Mr. Holmes, how would this chemical of yours affect satin?'

'It would not discolour the cloth, but would produce a visible stain.'

'I suggest, then, that we locate the gloves I noticed Mademoiselle Perrault wearing earlier this evening, and inspect them for stains.'

'How dare you?' the woman cried, racing for the door. But Lord Landsdowne got there first and braced himself against it to prevent her from leaving. Meanwhile, Lieutenant Breakstone quickly searched the room. As he peered behind a curtain near where Mme. Perrault had earlier been standing, he shouted: 'Here they are!'

'The game is up, Mademoiselle,' said Mycroft, a strangely satisfied smile on his face. 'Or, should I say, Fräulein.'

The kittenish façade vanished immediately from the young woman and her face became hard and cold.

'You may say whatever you like,' she answered in a low, emotionless voice which now bore no trace of a French accent, 'it will do nothing to bring back your King. The nicotine sulphate will act quickly. So, congratulations, Mr. Holmes, you have me. But you have lost the game. Your swinish sovereign is dead.'

Just then another voice filled the room. 'Swinish? Really, Marie, you have cut me to the quick,' it said, and I gasped to see His Majesty King Edward VII enter the room from a side door! 'They tried to warn me that you were a spy,' the King said with sadness, 'but I refused to believe it.'

As I stared at the silent figure in the bed, Mycroft Holmes (who seemed capable of reading thoughts) leaned over and said, 'On loan from Madame Tussaud's.'

'Would someone please tell me what is going on here?' John cried, but before anyone could answer, the faux Mlle. Perrault dashed to the pair of swords that adorned the wall and wrenched one loose. The blade whistled as she sliced it through the air and levelled its razor sharp point directly against His Majesty's throat! 'You shall not trick your way out of death this time!' she cried.

'Lieutenant, draw your weapon!' I demanded, but like everyone else in the room, he stood frozen, his face showing all too well the turmoil going on inside him.

'Madam,' he practically whimpered, 'how, as an Englishman, can I take arms against a woman?'

'Indeed,' Mlle. Perrault sneered, 'what fine English gentleman would lift a finger to harm a lady?'

'None,' I shouted, lunging for the crest

and pulling down the matching sword. 'For that you need a fine English woman! *En garde*, mademoiselle!'

I charged Mlle. Perrault, which at least forced her to remove the point from His Majesty's throat long enough to parry my thrust. Heavens, how many years had it been since I last held a sword? Not since old Laurence Delancey, the manager of my former theatrical troupe, had insisted that everyone in his company, even the women, learn the art of stage fencing. But fencing in the theatre and fighting for your life with a sword were worlds apart, as I was now learning.

Mlle. Perrault thrust her blade at me so relentlessly that all I could do was repeatedly sidestep its point, and what few effective parries I was able to make were more the result of accident than design. I expected to feel the sharp steel enter my flesh at any moment, and the fact that I did not rekindled my faith in Providence.

Unfortunately, Providence was not looking out for my beautiful new gown, which suffered a large gash at the hands of this Teutonic manifestation of Kali!

'My dress!' I cried, redoubling my efforts against my opponent. Underneath the loud clanking of blades I could hear John's panicked voice calling, 'For God's sake, Amelia, be careful!' Then, in my memory I heard another voice: that of Mr. Delancey proudly explaining a move of his own devising, designed to disarm the opponent — on stage, anyway. Still, what other options had I?

I continued to slash away, managing to parry thrust after thrust, waiting for my moment, which finally came when Mme. Perrault overextended herself on a lunge and momentarily lost her balance. As hard as I could, I beat at her blade from the right side, knowing she would counter-parry, then dipped under her sword and beat it again from the opposite direction, a move that served to weaken an opponent's grip. Then with a forward lunge I engaged her blade in an *envelopè*, encircling it once, twice, and on the third twirl, twisted my wrist around sharply, which wrenched the sword from her hand, sending it flying through the air. Her utter shock at being disarmed gave me ample opportunity to level the point of my blade at her midriff. Within a second, Sherlock Holmes had produced a set of handcuffs, and in quick order Mlle. Perrault was securely bound, though furiously cursing, and was escorted out of the room by Lord Landsdowne.

After my display of swashbuckling, the least I expected was a round of applause, but all I heard was John's plaintive voice crying: 'Would someone please tell me what in heaven's name this was about?'

Mycroft Holmes took the stage. 'Of course, Doctor. We had received intelligence from our agents abroad that a German spy whose mission was to scuttle the European peace pact had gained close access to His Majesty. We had a very good idea who it was, and an even better idea how she would accomplish her mission. If the King were to die, so would the *entente cordiale*. Since we had no actual proof to back up our suspicion, we could not arrest Mademoiselle Perrault. Such an act without the proper evidence could have resulted in an international incident with France, which would have jeopardized the *entente*. So you see the dilemma that faced us.

'It was finally decided to create a situation that would encourage her to take action. Earlier, Mrs. Watson, you charged me with being the instigator of this plan, but it was actually Sherlock who plotted out our little drama, which was predicated upon the assumption that Mademoiselle Perrault would be unable to resist taking advantage of our plan to make the King ill. We went so far as to provide her the opportunity by enlisting His Majesty's nine-year-old grandson to plant the firecracker. Needless to say, Sherlock did not actually inject His Majesty, but merely pretended to, catching the solution in a concealed sponge.'

John frowned. 'But wait a minute. That means that you had to know in advance that I would refuse to administer the dose,' he said.

Now Sherlock Holmes spoke up. 'You should know by now that I never sit down to a chess board without knowing in advance what moves my opponent will make. Your actions in particular, Watson, are as predictable as the tide.'

'Really, Holmes, you make me sound like a trained dog,' John complained (and about time!).

'I believe what my brother means, Doctor Watson,' Mycroft interjected, 'is that while we could not script your role to the extent we had for the *dramatis personae* present, we counted on your enviable loyalty to oath and Crown rendering you incapable of going through with our plan.'

'Very well,' I said, 'but why was it vital to involve John in this matter at all? Sir Francis could have done it equally well.'

'I am afraid it was necessary for the layering of the plot,' Mycroft answered. 'The success of our plan turned upon Mademoiselle Perrault's feeling secure in her deception every step of the way. Sir Francis Lacking is an important man in the palace, whose reputation is unimpeachable. He could not be brought down easily on charges of incompetence.'

'Whereas a humble private doctor could,' John said glumly.

'Look at it this way, old boy,' Sir Francis added, 'a second opinion is always desirable. My role in this was to verify, as another medical man, that the Perrault woman's plan had worked — or at least seemed to. But to make the mademoiselle secure enough in her success to walk into the trap, we had to produce someone expendable to take the blame.'

'Expendable!' I shouted.

'What Sir Francis undoubtedly meant was, someone who gave the illusion of being expendable,' Mycroft said soothingly.

'Well, Mr. Holmes,' I replied, testily, 'I only hope our humble, expendable selves performed our unwitting roles to your satisfaction.'

'May I say, madam, that you exceeded our expectations. I doubt any of us could have anticipated your fortuitous skill with a rapier.'

'Indeed!' the King cried out, and incredibly, I had all but forgotten his presence. 'How can we repay you? A reward? A title, perhaps?'

The answer came to me without even thinking. 'There is one thing Your Majesty could offer that would satisfy me.'

'Name it,' he said.

'An apology to my husband, who I fear

has been badly used in this affair.'

'That is all?' His Majesty asked, and I nodded. 'Then by all means! Doctor Watson, you have earned the profound thanks of the Crown, as well as our profound apology for any discomfort we have caused you.'

'Your Majesty, I — ' John began, but Mycroft interrupted him.

'Indeed, Doctor Watson, on behalf of the British government, I am truly sorry for what we have, by necessity, put you through, and offer my hand in friendship.'

'And I, sir,' added Lieutenant Breakstone, after which Sir Francis Lacking took John's hand and offered his apology. But after that there was a distinct silence.

'Well, Mr. Holmes?' I said.

Sherlock Holmes stiffened. 'Watson knows of my feelings for him.'

'I wish to hear you apologise,' I said.

'Yes, Holmes, be about it and let us get down to dinner,' His Majesty commanded

After shooting me a murderous look, Sherlock Holmes faced John and quietly said through clenched jaws, 'I am sorry, Watson.'

I was satisfied.

On our way back down to the ballroom, John whispered into my ear: 'By the way, where did you learn your prowess with a sword?'

'I will tell you later, darling,' I answered, then stepped away from him to pull aside Mycroft Holmes.

'Mr. Holmes, there is something yet bothering me,' I said. 'When you first telephoned us, you asked that I send away our maid before your arrival. How did you know we had a servant named Missy?'

'My dear Mrs. Watson, His Majesty depends upon my knowing things. I would not be overstating the matter to say that it is indeed my job.' Then, after giving me a stiff approximation of a bow, Mycroft Holmes lumbered inexorably towards the waiting banquet table.

The Adventure of
the Disappearing Coach

'Another letter from the doctor, ma'am,' Missy, our maid, announced brightly, as she flitted in and dropped the morning mail into my lap.

'Thank you, dear,' I muttered, eagerly tearing open the envelope from my husband, who had been gone near a fortnight, and whom I had been missing dreadfully. Unfolding the letter, I read, in familiar handwriting:

My dearest Amelia,

The reception in Leeds was even greater than that in Sheffield, which, as I mentioned in my last letter, was quite encouraging, to say the least. People everywhere in the kingdom seem to want to hear first-hand about my dealings with Sherlock Holmes. I am, of course, continuing to spread the news of Holmes's 'retirement', as he wished, and I am also happy to report that my podium style is improving with each lecture. On Friday I am off to York, which promises the largest audience yet. There has been talk about expanding the tour to another four cities

Heavens, *another* fortnight spent alone? If I thought Mr. Holmes's 'retirement' was going to translate into seeing more of my husband, I was in grievous error.

but I have discouraged such talk as I do not wish to tire myself. Neither do I want to spend the better part of the next month away from you, my dear.

Dear, sweet John! I held the letter close to my heart, a poor substitute for having John at home, though oddly comforting in its own way. Soon, however, curiosity about the other envelope Missy had delivered forced me to put aside my thoughts of him. This envelope was also addressed to me, though in a rough hand that I did not recognize. Inside, I discovered a ragged piece of card upon which a note was hastily (and not very properly) scrawled:

Amelia,

Im in trouble — their holding me at Scotland yard but I didnt do nothing. They dont beleve me. I need your help.

Harry Benbow.

Good heavens, Harry Benbow! What on earth had he got himself into this time? Even though we had only recently become reacquainted after an absence of some twenty years, I counted Harry as one of my closest friends. We had acted together with the Delancey Amateur Players when I was little more than a schoolgirl, and while it could be argued that I knew very little of his life since, I certainly knew him well enough to realize that he was no common criminal.

I read over the note again, searching for some indication that it was a product of Harry's characteristic sense of humour, but could discern none. The only clear message was that Harry was in trouble, and it was my duty as his friend to try and help him.

Although the rain had not yet begun to fall, a chilly mist permeated the air as I shivered on top of the bus (for no seats were available below) all the way to the imposing red-brick edifice of New Scotland Yard.

Marching inside, I requested to speak with a sergeant (or higher-up), and was directed to an overstuffed man with far more hair in his eyebrows than upon his head.

'I am Mrs. John H. Watson,' I announced, 'and I should like to be taken to Harry Benbow, who is falsely being held prisoner here.'

The sergeant's bushy brows furrowed as he regarded me, then his face brightened and he said, 'Oh, right: Benbow, the suspect in the Radford kidnapping case.'

'Kidnapping?' I cried. 'That is absurd. If Harry is a kidnapper, I am the Queen of Sheba. Who is in charge of the case? Inspector Laurie?'

'No ma'am, Inspector Carrigan's the man on that one; but if I was you, I wouldn't go sounding off to him. He's not in much of a mood for it, with the newspapers on his back and all.'

Suddenly I made the connection between an article that had appeared in the *Times* a day or two back and poor Harry's predicament. The article had detailed the disappearance of the two young sons of a wealthy businessman living in Mayfair, and the subsequent ransom note asking for, if memory served, £50,000.

'I would be grateful if I could see Inspector Carrigan at once,' I said. 'It is important.'

After being ushered through a seemingly endless maze of desks and offices, I finally arrived at a cramped cubbyhole inhabited by a dark-complexioned man who appeared to be asleep in his chair.

'Pardon me, sir,' the sergeant said, 'but here's a woman who says she has information on the Radford case.'

The man opened one eye, and regarded me somewhat suspiciously before inflicting daylight upon his other eye.

'I suppose you had better tell me, then,' he grumbled. 'Who are you and what do you know?'

'My name is Amelia Watson, and I know that you are holding the wrong man as a suspect,' I said.

At that, Inspector Carrigan broke out with a harsh, snorting laugh that conveyed very little mirth. 'Oh, we've got the wrong man, have we? And I suppose that evidence we found on him is the wrong evidence, too.'

'What evidence?'

The inspector leaned back in his chair and surveyed me from head to toe and back again, a gesture I find rude and demeaning in the extreme. 'Just what is your interest in this case?' he asked.

'I am a friend of Harry Benbow's,' I said, coolly. 'May I sit down?'

'As you wish,' he said, and I took the only seat available in the office.

'Now then, please tell me what evidence you have against Harry.'

After ingesting a pinch of snuff, he began: 'Well, it seems the younger of the two boys has this toy, a stuffed bear doll that's called a Neddy, or Teddy, or something like that. It was sent over from the States by some American business partner of Andrew Radford — he's the boys' father — and when the boy disappeared, the doll disappeared too, which says to us that he must have had it with him. But then up pops this Harry Benbow, and guess what he's holding?'

'The bear?'

'Right. Both Mr. and Mrs. Radford positively identified it. So you tell me: if Benbow isn't the kidnapper, how did he get that toy?'

I had to admit that it did not sound good for Harry. Still, I could not accept that he would have anything to do with such a horrible crime. 'May I see Harry?' I asked.

'No, you may not,' he answered, with finality.

It was becoming obvious that mere persistence was not going to budge this man, so I decided upon a different — if somewhat shameless — tactic. Pulling out my handkerchief, I began to dab at my eyes while sobbing: 'Poor Harry, I hate to think of him in that horrible cell, all alone, with no one to talk to.'

It took the production of nearly as much rainfall from my eyes as was now pittering into the Thames outside, but eventually Inspector Carrigan relented. 'Oh, crikey, go and see him then!' he cried. 'Just stop that blubbering!'

'Thank you,' I twittered, dashing out of the office before my sobs began to sound too much like stifled laughter.

Minutes later, I was being escorted by the sergeant down to a ghastly row of holding cells, so bleak and foreboding that I shivered as I walked through.

We stopped at the very last cell, the door of which was unlocked by the warder. Inside, looking confused and defeated, was the diminutive figure of Harry Benbow.

'Amelia!' he shouted as soon as he saw me. 'Thank heaven you've come!'

'What have you done now, Harry?' I asked.

'Gor, I wish I knew! One minute I'm minding my own business, and in the next I'm being accused o' pinching some Mayfair toff's kiddies! Or maybe I should say, his *toff*-spring.' He waggled his eyebrows and grinned.

'Don't joke, Harry,' I said, laughing in spite of myself. 'We have to find a way to get you out of here.'

'Right, so here's what we do: you put your friend Sherlock Holmes on the case, he finds the real kidnapper, and I'm out o' here before you can say Bob's your uncle!'

I sighed. 'So that was why you wanted me to come. Harry, Mr. Holmes has gone away, and I cannot contact him.'

Harry turned pale. 'Gone away?'

'I am sorry,' I added, helplessly. 'But why don't you tell me what happened, and maybe I can find some way to help.'

'Alright. I've told everyone else 'round here, but none o' them believes me. See, for the past month or so I've been doing a little busking — not because I have to, mind you, but just to keep in practice. Anyway, I settled into a spot near the Tower Bridge. There's a good crowd o' people down there, and I'm giving 'em some o' the old songs, a few dances, some patter, you know. Then one day, as I'm stepping out for a pint and a bit o' fish, I see this coach come tearing around the corner like the Devil himself was driving it, and coming from inside is the sound of some poor little tyke crying his eyes out. Then I see this thing come flying out the coach window, so I go over to look, and it's this little bear cub toy. I reckon the little duck's lost his toy, and that's why he's so upset. So I start to run after the coach to return it, and it turns onto a dead-end street. But by the time I get there, the coach, horse, and screaming tyke are now all inside some big shed, and as I'm running towards it, the driver closes the doors. Then . . . '

'Go on, Harry.'

'Then I run up to the building, but the door's locked from the inside, so I peek inside the window . . . and there's nothing there, Amelia.'

'Nothing?'

'No coach, no horse, no driver, no crying tyke. Nothing.'

'Could they have got out another way?'

'I would've seen 'em. They just disappeared. So I says to myself, 'Harry,

45

you got two choices: you can go barking just thinking about it, or you can go back to work.' So I go back to work, but now I've got this sweet little bear, and I decide I might as well work it into the act. So I start feeding the bear straight lines, and throwing my voice into it for the laughs. And it's going great with the crowds. Next thing I know, there's this peeler, and he's getting really interested in the bear. I'm thinking he likes the jokes, but before you can say Bob's yer uncle, there's a whole circle of 'em standing 'round me, and before I know it I'm brought down here and tossed in the clink. This Inspector Carrigan bloke, he just keeps demanding to know where those two boys are hidden, and he won't even listen to my story.'

'And he is naturally under pressure to find the missing boys,' I muttered. 'Harry, I think I might be able to get you out of here. It may not work, but it is worth a try.' I then called for the warder, who took a leisurely amount of time opening the door, and asked to be taken once more to Inspector Carrigan.

'Well, Mrs. Watson,' he said as I re-entered his office, 'you seem to have regained your composure. Did you have a nice chat with Benbow?'

'Yes,' I said, quietly, 'and I feel I owe you an apology.'

'Indeed?'

'I did not believe you, but talking with Harry, I came to realize that he must be guilty.' I dabbed at my eyes again. 'I feel so betrayed. I only wish there was something more I could do to help you.'

The inspector leaned across his desk in a conspiratorial fashion. 'You'd be willing to help us, eh? Do you think he'd tell you where the boys are?'

'I don't know. But listen, I had a thought on the way back here: what if Harry was released and then his movements were tracked? He might lead us straight to the children.'

'He might run, too.'

'Not with me watching him,' I replied. 'He trusts me; my presence would not be a threat to him.'

'No, it sounds too risky.'

'Inspector, think of those two poor

boys. What if they have been left alone? What if something dreadful were to happen to them while Harry was being held as a suspect? Think of the public outcry!'

Inspector Carrigan snorted again, and I sensed that he was indeed thinking.

'Alright,' he said, 'if you can guarantee me that you'll keep a watch on him, I'll release the little devil. I'll have the papers ready tomorrow morning. But in return, I expect to get reports of his every move, or else it's your pretty head in the noose.'

'I understand,' I said, 'and I will do anything to see that Harry gets what he deserves.'

Taking my leave of Scotland Yard, I returned home to Queen Anne Street, weary from the strange and trying day, but knowing that there was little time to waste.

Having achieved my objective of getting Harry released from that horrible cell, I now had to figure out how to free him from constant police scrutiny. By the time the evening clock chimed ten, my plan was formulated.

It was audacious, almost laughable, and perhaps it was simply the lateness of the hour, but I was convinced it would work.

I spent most of the next morning setting the plan in action, then travelled once more to Scotland Yard, in order to retrieve Harry. As we two were being marched out of the premises by Inspector Carrigan and a covey of constables, I managed to whisper to Harry the basics of my plan.

Our procession went without incident until we were outside the massive iron gate, at which point Harry shouted: 'You traitor!' and, with a powerful shove, pushed me down onto the pavement.

Police whistles pierced the air as a circle of constables stood round me, trying to help. I watched as Harry darted in and out of the crowds on the Embankment eluding the police. A few moments later, a breathless constable reappeared to inform the inspector, 'He's gone, sir, he jumped into a cab and it sped away.'

'Well, try to find it!' Inspector Carrigan roared, and a dozen constables rushed away. Then he turned on me. 'Look what you have caused, madam!'

'I am sorry,' I panted, 'but I fear I am also hurt. Please help me up.'

As the remaining constables helped me to my feet, I heard a voice call out: 'Heavens, child, is that you?' and saw what appeared to be a small, white-haired woman rushed towards me.

'Now who's this?' Inspector Carrigan demanded.

'Jemima Pratt,' the figure answered, 'a family friend, you might say. How fortunate 'tis that I happened to be passing this way. Are you hurt, love?'

'I am not sure,' I answered honestly.

'Come home with me, dear, I'll make you some tea.'

I looked to the inspector who grumbled, 'Fine, fine, get out of here.'

After hailing a cab, we quickly got in and sped away. 'I hope that wasn't too hard of a shove, ducks,' my companion said, in a different voice entirely.

'It had to be convincing, Harry,' I said, watching him pull off the grey wig and start to unbutton the black dress that had transformed him into the convincing model of an old woman. I only hoped the rest of the charade was as convincing.

'But 'Jemima Pratt'? I thought we agreed you would be John's former landlady, Martha Hudson. Those clothes were borrowed from her, after all.'

'Right you are, ducks, but you know my 'istory,' Harry said. 'I gets everyone I know in trouble eventually. If I'd a' said I was Martha Hudson, who knows? The real Martha Hudson mighta found 'erself in clink by supper time, and I'd hate to get such a nice ol' gal in the soup.'

I wish I could have disagreed with his logic, but I knew Harry too well. As it turned out, the real Martha Hudson (who looked nothing like Jemima Pratt) greeted us at the door of 221B Baker Street, where I had dispatched the hansom, and I once more thanked her profusely for the loan of the clothes, which had been placed inside the cab that I had retained for the sole purpose of spiriting Harry away and facilitating his quick change. Mrs. Hudson accepted this bizarre affair with a sense of amusement (I imagine that, over the years, she must have become accustomed to all manner of strangeness) and further displayed her angelic nature by agreeing to put up Harry, in the now-empty rooms that had once housed Sherlock Holmes, until this business was concluded.

It seemed clear that the only way to exonerate Harry was to find the missing boys ourselves. I was convinced that Harry had indeed seen the kidnapper's fleeing coach, but refused to believe it had simply disappeared into thin air. 'Tell me everything again, Harry,' I said, pacing the floor of the empty (and now somehow soulless) apartment, and he repeated his story, but it still made no sense. After a day of searching for answers, we retired, exhausted. Leaving Harry to the able care of Mrs. Hudson, I returned home.

I was awakened from a late sleep the next morning by Missy, who informed me that another letter from John had arrived. Without rising from the bed (my hip was still sore from yesterday's adventure), I tore open the envelope and read:

Dearest;

I must report a singular occurrence that took place at last night's lecture. While looking out at the audience I was suddenly struck by the appearance of an elderly gentleman who was regarding me with great intensity. My initial reaction was to shout: 'Holmes!' for so I thought it was, in one of his disguises. Seeing the man so distracted me that I momentarily lost track of my speech, and by the time I looked up from my notes, he was retreating through the back door. Had it really been he? Or am I just so involved with the man and his exploits that I am seeing apparitions of him? Or was this visitation simply borne of my desire to see Holmes again, a way of trying to force the very ground that has seemingly opened up and swallowed him to reveal him once more. I must confess, Amelia, that I am still struggling with the idea of his not being within reach.

I finished the letter and set it next to its cherished brethren on the table beside the bed, and went about my morning routine. It was while I was dressing that the words from John's letter struck me, and suddenly Harry's story did not seem so ridiculous.

I set out for Baker Street at once, stopping on the way at a stationer's to buy a street map, which I carried into the empty rooms and unfolded on the floor before Harry. 'Show me where you were when you saw the coach,' I asked.

He pointed to a spot on the South Bank near the Tower Bridge. 'Right around here, near Pickle Herring street.'

'Yet the children were abducted from Mayfair, which is all the way over here. Why transport them across the river to that place in particular?'

'Maybe he fancies himself a bit of old Dickie the Third, you know, locking up the young princes in the Tower o' London?'

'No, there's another reason, and to prove it we must find that building that opened up and swallowed the carriage.'

Despite the grim, grey sky, the streets remained dry as we travelled by cab virtually the entire length of the city and across the London Bridge, before finally disembarking on Tooley Street near London Bridge Station. 'This way,' Harry said, leading me down an alleyway, at the end of which stood a large, drab building.

'There it is,' he called, and we rushed towards it, only to find that the large, barn-style doors were held fast by a padlock. Obviously the mysterious tenant was out, having locked the door behind him.

'We need to get inside here,' I said, examining the front of the building.

'Well, ducks, I figure either we can break that window over there and climb through, risking life and limb, or you can loan me a hairpin,' Harry answered.

'A hairpin? Are you serious?'

He grinned back at me. ''Course I am. Didn't I ever tell you my dear ol' Da was a locksmith?'

I handed him the pin and, true to his word, the lock was open and on the ground within a minute. The building was dark, but not so dark that we could not make out a strange cage-like box that occupied most of the interior. 'That wasn't there when I peeped through the shutters,' Harry said, fingering one of the steel walls. 'What is it?'

'Unless I have become completely addled, it is a lift, probably designed to raise and lower building materials. It is certainly big enough to hold a two-wheeled coach and horse, and the reason you did not see it before is because it was descending when you looked in.'

'But who in blazes would want to go under the ground . . . *Gor!*' Harry said, slapping his forehead with his palm. 'Half o' blinkin' London back in the day, that's who.'

'Yes, Harry, the same realization came to me this morning, but I had to make sure I was right. This must be the lowering mechanism,' I said, touching a loop of rope that ran through a pulley on the ceiling and then disappeared through a hole cut into the floor of the lift. We both took hold of the rope and pulled, though the platform dropped so easily that I could have managed it alone. We descended into what should have been darkness, but someone had thoughtfully placed oil lanterns in niches carved into the walls of the shaft at various intervals.

Before long we bumped to a stop, and

in the dim light of the lanterns I could see a wide passageway containing an open bale of hay (as well as other, less pleasant, traces of a horse's recent inhabitation) and lengths of huge iron pipes. Directly behind us was a more nostalgic sight: the wide spiral staircase that provided street access to this underground thoroughfare. We were in the Tower Subway, a pedestrian tunnel running under the Thames that had been closed upon the opening of the Tower Bridge some ten years ago, and eventually forgotten. Although somebody had obviously remembered it.

'You think the tykes are in the subway?' Harry asked.

'If they are not, I'll eat that hay bale,' I said, as we stepped onto a wooden platform that had been erected over the water mains that the tunnel now housed. We had travelled only a few yards over the planking, past the first great arch of the tunnel, when I heard a young voice call out: 'He's coming back!'

Following the voice, I ran to the next arch and was greeted by a sight that nearly shattered my heart. In the midst of a dirty, makeshift camp were the two boys, their faces pale and haggard and their eyes were rimmed with fear. A sob rose up in my throat upon seeing that the brute who had brought them down into this dank netherworld had also left them tied up in their chairs with ropes that visibly chafed their wrists and ankles.

'Please don't hurt us,' the younger of the two said in a tiny, frightened voice.

'No, darling,' I said, rushing to him and smothering his brow with kisses, insufficient compensation for his ordeal.

'Who are you?' the elder boy asked.

'We are friends who have come to get you out of here,' I assured him. 'When will your captor return?'

'Soon,' the same one replied. 'He usually leaves this time of day, but he comes back quickly.'

Harry had already begun to saw through the ropes with a penknife. When he had released the younger boy, he said, 'I'll bet you're the one who lost his little bear.'

The boy's face instantly lit up. 'You've found my Teddy?'

'Keeping it safe just for your return,'

58

Harry said, and, taking the younger boy's hand while I took that of his brother, we started back towards the lift. A voice from the shadows, however, stopped us.

'Well, well, well,' Inspector Carrigan said, raising his revolver, 'both the conspirators and their prey are found in the warren.'

'I'm glad to see you, Inspector,' I said. 'We have found the boys.'

'And I have found you. Come over here, lads.' Reluctantly, the boys joined him on his side of the revolver, which unfortunately was still trained on Harry and me. 'Recovering the missing children and capturing the kidnappers, not a bad day's work,' he gloated.

The older of the two boys cried: 'They are not — ' but the inspector cut him off, saying:

'Shush now, lad, I have the situation in hand.' Then, turning to me, he sneered: 'You really must have thought I was just another ruddy stupid copper, like the ones in those worthless detective stories people write. But I didn't believe you for a second, madam. I had a tail on you from the moment you left the Yard, and I knew that sooner or later you and your friend here would lead us to the boys. So why don't we all go topside, real quiet like. And don't even think about trying to escape again, because I've got men surrounding this building.'

Inspector Carrigan then motioned us onto the lift with his revolver, and instructed Harry and me to operate the pulley, which was considerably more difficult for the journey upwards, particularly in light of the three extra bodies on board (and I could only wonder at the level of strength required to raise the platform with a horse and coach!). By the half-way point my strength was spent, and it was up to Harry to bring us to the surface. But even before we arrived, we could hear the sounds of chaos taking place just above our heads.

As we broke through into daylight, we were greeted by the sight of two police constables struggling mightily with a large, burly man dressed in the garb of a cabman, just outside the doors of the shed.

One of the constables addressed Inspector Carrigan. 'We found this man snooping around the building, sir. He took one look at us and tried to run, but we got him. He's a strong one, though!'

'That's him!' cried the younger boy. 'That's the one who took us!'

'What? What's that?' the inspector muttered, trying to follow the line of confusion.

At that very moment another man appeared, and only the unexpected presence of my husband would have been a more welcome sight.

'Alright, Carrigan, you have me here,' Sir Melville Macnaghten bristled, 'now, what is it that is so beastly important?'

While I could not claim to know Sir Melville well, he was an ally of John's, and I had been a guest at the dinner party celebrating his ascension to the post of Assistant Commissioner of the Criminal Investigation Division.

'I wanted you to be here when I solved the Radford case, sir,' the inspector said; and, pointing at us, added: 'These two are the kidnappers.'

Sir Melville glanced at me and then did a 'take' that would have done Harry proud. 'Mrs. Watson, is it not?' he said.

'What are you doing here?'

'It will take a long time to explain, Sir Melville,' I said, 'but you have no idea how happy I am to see you.'

The inspector eyed us warily. 'You know each other?'

'Of course we do,' Sir Melville replied, 'her husband has helped out the Yard on many occasions. A kidnapper, you say? You must be daft, man!' Then a smile softened his face. 'Ah, but these must be the missing boys. Glad to have you back, lads.'

He then turned to the still-struggling cabman. 'Who is this?'

'I . . . don't know, sir,' Inspector Carrigan said sickly. 'My men caught him sneaking around.'

'Me name's Hoskins, an' I drive a hack, that's all,' the man declared.

'He is the blackguard who took us away!' the older boy cried, and Hoskins countered the boy's defiance with a murderous look.

Meanwhile, the younger one dashed in front of Harry and me, as though to protect us, and cried: 'And this man and this lady are the ones who found us. They are not criminals!'

'I see,' Sir Melville said. 'So Mrs. Watson and her friend discovered the whereabouts of the missing boys, while the foot constables managed to capture the kidnapper. Tell me, Carrigan; what, exactly, was your participation in this effort?'

The inspector's mouth worked up and down, though no sound came out. He was still attempting to speak as Sir Melville instructed a half-dozen of his officers to take the villainous Hoskins to the Yard. Then, kneeling down to face the boys, Sir Melville said, 'I wish my men were half as brave as you lads. But now we must get you home to your parents.'

As the two boys ran to the police carriage, Inspector Carrigan finally found his voice. 'Sir, I would like to say — '

'You may say whatever you like this afternoon in my office, Carrigan,' Sir Melville snapped. 'Now then, Mrs. Watson and Mr . . . '

'Benbow, sir,' Harry said.

'Mr. Benbow. May I offer you the

63

comfort of my carriage back to Scotland Yard? I am afraid we still must trouble you both for your statements.'

Our last view of Inspector Carrigan as we drove away was of him throwing his bowler hat to the ground and stomping it as though it were a snake.

In the carriage, Harry asked: 'How do you think this Hoskins bloke even knew about the lift in the subway?'

'I am sure we will learn upon questioning him,' Sir Melville said, 'though I could not help but notice the man's hands. They were quite scarred, and several of his fingernails were discoloured and misshapen, not the sort of marks one normally sees on the hands of a hackney driver. They are more indicative of a labourer, particularly one who works with heavy tools. A sandhog, for instance, or perhaps a pipe fitter.'

'Are you saying that he might have worked on the crew that installed the water pipes in the subway?' I asked.

'It is a theory, nothing more,' Sir Melville responded.

'*Gor*,' said Harry, 'if I didn't know

better, I'd swear I was in the presence o' Sherlock Holmes himself!'

The smile of satisfaction was still on Sir Melville's face when we reached New Scotland Yard.

The Adventure of
the Georgian Deed

'Have another scone, dear,' the plumpish, grey-haired woman said, nudging the plate in my direction.

'Heavens, Martha, one more and I will positively burst,' I replied, 'though I will take a drop more tea, if you please.'

Martha Hudson, my husband's former landlady, refilled my cup as we both watched the cold November rain patter against the window. This was our third tea in as many weeks, since we had both recently found ourselves alone. My husband, Dr. John H. Watson, was still touring the provinces with a staged reading that recounted his adventures alongside his friend Sherlock Holmes (which, according to a friend who had attended his performance in Bath, were beginning to make the exploits of Sir Gawain seem commonplace by comparison).

As for Holmes, he had vacated 221B Baker Street in order to pursue a ring of devilish international criminals, under the guise of retirement, leaving Mrs. Hudson without her primary tenant. Not surprisingly, our teatime conversations frequently centred around John and his former flatmate, and I quickly discovered that Mrs. Hudson was a fount of information and remembrances. She was, in fact, in the middle of one such when a sharp knock sounded at the front door.

'Who could that be?' she wondered, and I could read on her face the faint hope that it might be the great detective himself, returning from his self-imposed exile.

Instead of Mr. Holmes, however, the caller turned out to be a man of thirty or less, with brown, doe-like eyes, and a perpetually startled look that I quickly realized was not so much expression as the fall of his features.

'Mr. Holmes, please,' the man said, shaking the sleety rain from his hat while clutching to his chest a small black leather case.

'I am sorry, sir, but Mr. Holmes is no longer here,' Mrs. Hudson said.

The man's eyes widened in panic. 'No longer here?' he cried. 'But I am in urgent need of his assistance. Where has he gone?'

'Retired,' Mrs. Hudson said, though she knew the truth regarding Mr. Holmes's disappearance as well as I. Her next statement, however, caught me completely by surprise: 'Perhaps, in Mr. Holmes's absence, you could relate your problem to Mrs. Amelia Watson. She has conducted quite a few investigations of her own.'

I turned upon Martha with a look of horror, wondering if this was a demonstration of some hitherto unseen sense of whimsy, but her pleasant, open face was free of any guile.

I turned to the stranger. 'Sir,' I began, 'I am afraid — ' But he interrupted me with the remark: 'Watson . . . are you by any chance related to Dr. Watson?'

'By marriage,' I answered. 'He is my husband.'

'I see. He might be able to help me, given his association with Mr. Holmes, but I fail to see how you could, being a woman.'

I glared at the wide-eyed young boor dripping rainwater on Mrs. Hudson's floor, and heard myself declare: 'It so happens that I assisted Scotland Yard in the apprehension of the Mayfair Kidnapper only last month, in addition to having worked with my husband, and Sherlock Holmes, *and* the Metropolitan police force on numerous cases involving crime and investigation. And furthermore — '

'Perhaps we should discuss it by the fire, dear,' Mrs. Hudson suggested, taking the man's dripping greatcoat and hat, then ushering him into her sitting room and the seat closest to the hearth. A twinkling smile from the landlady encouraged me to cool my emotions as our visitor warmed his body.

Once thawed, the man introduced himself as Ralph Montfort and, to his credit, apologised for his earlier rudeness. 'I just did not know where else to turn, except to Sherlock Holmes,' he said.

'There are other personal detectives in London,' I offered.

'True, but only one Sherlock Holmes,' Mr. Montfort said. Once more, John's literary skills had spoken for him, having seeded in yet another mind the conviction that a visit to Sherlock Holmes was all that was necessary to solve any human ill, from poverty to baldness. Still, the man did appear to be in need of some help.

'What exactly is troubling you, Mr. Montfort?' I asked.

He leaned forward in Mrs. Hudson's best chair, and began.

'For as long as I can remember, I have heard stories about a lost treasure within the Montfort family: some object of great importance and value, now lost to history. I will not go into the legend, since it is quite fanciful, except to say that family tradition holds that the object carries with it a deadly curse.' He paused before adding: 'I believe I have found it.'

'Indeed? What is it?' I asked.

He glanced nervously at Mrs. Hudson, who picked up on his discomfort and excused herself to refill the teapot. Once she had pottered away, he clumsily opened his case and withdrew a folder, from which he produced a single piece of parchment, which he set on the small coffee table.

'I did not find it myself, my brother did,' he said. 'It was hidden behind a painting in my father's library.'

I could make out little of the writing on the document, though the crimson wax seal signified great import. More clear was the signature beside the seal, and my eyes widened as I read the name of George II!

'What is this?' I gasped.

'A land deed, signed by the King himself,' he replied. 'It decrees that seven hundred acres of land in Tilbury shall be deeded to Sir Robert Montfort as of the date of the document, September 12, 1752, as payment of a debt. This means that my family has been the legal owners of an entire estate of land for over one hundred and fifty years, without even knowing about it.'

'But why would someone accept such a deed, then put it away and forget about it?'

'The legend tells of Sir Robert

71

engaging in a fight to the death with a cousin, who wished to usurp his title and property. The curse, it is said, was uttered by Sir Robert on his deathbed, against the cousin — that all who attempt to hold the treasure, save for the rightful owner, shall die. After Robert's own death, the treasure — this deed — disappears from history. I can only speculate that the usurping cousin, whomever he was, hid it out of fear of the curse.'

With great care, I picked up the parchment. 'I am afraid I know little about ancient documents,' I admitted. 'Has this been authenticated?'

'It has. My brother took care of that. Right before he was murdered.'

'Murdered?'

Mrs. Hudson returned with a fresh pot of tea, and poured a cup for our visitor.

'My brother Matthew was found in my father's library, strangled,' Mr. Montfort added, a declaration that nearly caused Mrs. Hudson to drop the tea-tray. 'The room showed signs of having been searched.'

'Do you have any idea who might have been responsible?' I asked.

Staring at the tea swirling in his cup, the young man shook his head. 'No,' he said quietly, though hardly convincingly. Clearly he knew, or at least suspected, more than he was admitting.

I tried another approach. 'Who else knows about the discovery of the deed?'

'The document expert who examined it, a Mr. Rowley, is the only party I know of. I have taken care to tell no one else, but I fear my brother was not so reticent. The truth is, I have no idea who might know about it. I have no idea who might be following me, watching me, waiting for the proper moment to cause me harm and steal the deed. That is why I have moved from my home to temporary lodgings.'

'But who would wish to steal it?' I asked. 'It seems clear that only a member of the Montfort family could claim the property. Could it be that a member of your own family is behind the plot?'

'I am the last of the Montforts,' he stated. 'But if I were to die before I am able to make a claim on the property, the deed will be nullified and the present landowners will simply maintain their holdings as though nothing had ever arisen to challenge them.'

'So you suspect that the current land-holders are aware of your discovery and are responsible for your brother's death?'

His face dropped down and he muttered, 'I did not say that.' Ralph Montfort was a very poor liar.

'What do you plan to do now?' I inquired.

'I was rather hoping Mr. Holmes would tell me.'

'I am certain he would tell you to consult the police.'

'Oh, I could hardly do that, since the police are part of . . . that is, I prefer not to involve the police.' He rose and reached for his coat and hat. 'If that is truly your best advice, I shall accept it and be off. But if you hear from Mr. Holmes, please contact me. I am staying at the Sturridge Hotel, but if I find it necessary to leave there, I will let you know of my whereabouts.'

'Mr. Montfort, please wait,' I said, stopping him at the door. 'If you feel uncomfortable with the police, perhaps I could do something to help you, at least until Mr. Holmes returns.'

He eyed me warily.

'Such as . . . ?'

'Well, perhaps I could research the document for you. You have been relying on family tradition for information, but perhaps there is a recorded history of the deed.'

'That certainly would help the claim of authenticity,' he said.

'It is settled then,' I affirmed. 'Might I hold onto the deed for purposes of study?'

Ralph Montfort shook his head. 'No, I cannot take the chance of letting it out of my possession. I have, however, written out a copy of the text.' Reaching into his case, he pulled out a sheet of paper upon which he had copied the deed and handed it to me. 'If you do discover something, you will contact me immediately?'

'Of course,' I replied, and with that, Ralph Montfort returned to the grey, wet streets of London from whence he had come. Only after he had gone did I realize that I had not the slightest notion of how to begin such an undertaking as researching a royal document.

Since I wanted to return home before the darkness and gloom became impenetrable, I took leave of 221 Baker Street soon thereafter. Even though it was a reasonable walking distance from my home in Queen Anne Street, the night chill and rain forced me to seek out a cab. By good fortune, an unoccupied hansom was standing by the kerb, as though waiting for me, and I dashed inside. But as it drove away, I noticed a man standing on the street, seemingly oblivious to the rain, and paying what I considered undue attention to me. His face was coarse and pockmarked, and with growing alarm I noticed that his dark, probing eyes followed the path of the cab until distance intervened.

My relief at leaving the man behind was short lived, however, as it quickly became clear the cabman had interests other than depositing me at my home. 'You have missed the turn,' I shouted to the driver as we careened past Portman

Square, but the driver ignored me. We continued on for several minutes at a reckless canter, and eventually the vehicle turned onto Piccadilly. Clearly, I was being taken somewhere, but where, and for what reason?

At last we came to a stop in front of an imposing building on Pall Mall and the driver stepped down. 'Where have you brought me?' I demanded, refusing to take his proffered hand, preferring to struggle down to the pavement without help. He only smiled apologetically and said, 'All will be explained inside.'

At the door of the strange building I was greeted by a stiff, pale butler who handed me, of all things, a man's coat and hat!

'Please put these on, madam,' he intoned.

'I will do no such thing!' I rejoined, but his quiet insistence told me that I would not be allowed past him without engaging in this ridiculous charade.

'Very well,' I muttered, jamming the hat down over my head, 'but there had better be an excellent explanation for this!'

Once in mannish outerwear, I was rushed through the lobby of the building, obviously a gentleman's club, the center of which boasted a bronze statue of Diogenes holding forth his lantern (presumably to guide his way through the thick layer of cigar smoke that fogged the room). I was hustled to a private lift and carried to an upper floor, then taken to a private apartment. I waited while the butler gingerly knocked on the door. 'Enter,' a voice behind the door called — a voice I recognized.

The enormous figure of Mycroft Holmes, the elder brother of Sherlock, was so deeply rooted into a leather chair that I thought perhaps only surgery could have separated the two. But he managed to rise as I came into the room.

'Good evening, Mrs. Watson,' he said, with a courtly nod. 'You have the distinction of being the first woman ever to set foot inside the Diogenes Club. Chatterton, take Mrs. Watson's coat and hat then leave us, please.'

The butler did so.

'Well, Mr. Holmes, if I must be kidnapped, I am at least glad it was by someone with whom I am acquainted. I trust His Majesty is well?'

'Quite, and he sends his regards.' I had learned during my first experience with Mycroft Holmes, some months earlier, that his position within the British government went far beyond ordinary civil servitude. Motioning me into a chair, he sank back into his own and asked: 'May I offer you something?'

'Indeed you may. An explanation.'

Mycroft Holmes smiled. 'It has come to my attention that earlier this evening, you were in the company of one Ralph Montfort.'

News seemed to travel on the wind whenever Mycroft Holmes is involved. 'Yes, I was,' I replied. 'Mr. Montfort appeared at 221B seeking your brother. I happened to be there.'

'Very fortunate for us,' he said, pouring himself a brandy from a wheeled cart that was stationed beside his chair. 'And no doubt Mr. Montfort told you about a certain land grant that he had discovered.'

'Yes, he showed it to me. It covers some acreage in Tilbury.'

The broad face of Mycroft Holmes darkened. 'You saw the document?'

'Yes, though I was unable to make out much of the writing. What is this about, Mr. Holmes?'

Swirling his brandy, then draining the snifter in one gulp, he said: 'What this is about, Mrs. Watson, is the potential economic crippling of Great Britain. That acreage in Tilbury is not just an innocuous parcel of property, it is land fronting the Thames. More specifically, Mr. Montfort's claim purports ownership of property that currently holds the largest and busiest shipping ports in the nation.'

'I see.'

'Do you, Mrs. Watson? Let me emphasize the point. If it were indeed proven that Ralph Montfort was the rightful owner of this land, he would have the legal power to charge any price for its use, or even close the docks altogether, should he so desire. The entire British shipping industry would be disrupted. Imports of grain and coal would slow to a mere trickle. Think what would happen to the price of goods once the world had learned that England's port facilities had been crippled. A nation desperate for coal would be forced to pay any price to get it. England would no longer be the seat of a great empire, but a weakened nation, praying that it has more allies in the world than aggressors. All because of an alleged deed drawn by a Hanoverian monarch.' He slammed the brandy glass down on the cart, which caused me to jump.

'You have left me speechless, Mr. Holmes,' I managed to utter.

'Oh, I do apologise,' he said, smiling again. 'At times I get carried away. But I am sure you will understand that all of us in Whitehall and Buckingham Palace will rest much more easily if it can be proven that the document is a forgery. For that reason, we must scrutinize it.'

'But it has been examined already,' I said.

'Yes, we know all about that. In fact, it was a letter sent to the Prime Minister by one Thomas Rowley that first alerted us to this problem. Rowley, apparently an expert on old parchments, wrote that he had seen and authenticated such a land deed, signed by King George the second.'

'Have you talked with this Mr. Rowley?'

'We did try. Unfortunately, when our man arrived at Mr. Rowley's office, he found an unhappy sight. Mr. Rowley, it seems, had been strangled.'

I gasped, and blurted out: 'Like Mr. Montfort's brother!'

'His brother, you say?'

I related the tale as had been told by Ralph Montfort, dismissing the story of the curse as legend, while emphasizing that he seemed to know more about his pursuers than he was acknowledging.

Then a horrible thought gripped my mind: if the property in question was controlled by the British government for use as dockland, could it be Parliament, or even the Crown itself that was responsible for the death of Matthew Montfort, and the pursuit of his brother?

'You appear disturbed, Mrs. Watson?' I heard Mr. Holmes saying.

'Oh, I am sorry. It is just the intrigue of this evening catching up with me.'

'I understand,' he nodded, 'and based

on your own testimony regarding Mont-fort's brother, this intrigue is taking a decidedly dangerous turn. I must admit, we had not counted on there being a third party striving to possess the deed. Mrs. Watson, I am going to ask you for a small favour. Please contact Mr. Montfort and tell him that you have spoken with Mr. Holmes, which, indeed, you have. Tell him that Mr. Holmes will meet him at 221B tomorrow — no, make that day after tomorrow — at seven o'clock in the evening. Would you do that?'

'Yes, I suppose,' I answered.

'Good. Our experts will be there, ready to examine the document. Now, after you have done so, I implore you to forget you ever met a man named Ralph Montfort, and forget you ever saw the land deed. It is simply too dangerous to involve yourself further in this matter.'

'It almost sounds, Mr. Holmes, as though you too know more about this affair than you are letting on.'

'Not at all,' he said, pouring another brandy, 'it is simply that I would feel very bad if anything were to happen to you.

Good evening, Mrs. Watson, and thank you.' He then tugged on a bell cord and within moments, Chatterton reappeared at the door, brandishing the same ridiculous coat and bowler hat that I had worn in.

'I have one more question, Mr. Holmes,' I said, as I donned the heavy coat and stuffed my hair under the hat, 'what if the deed is genuine?'

'In that case, we shall be forced to buy it from Mr. Montfort at whatever price he quotes.'

'And if he refuses to sell?'

Mr. Holmes smiled again, but the expression now seemed cheerless and forced. 'Good evening, Mrs. Watson,' he said.

I was ushered out of the building and into another waiting cab. The chill that was coursing through my body was not simply a result of the weather. I had no doubt that it had been Mycroft's shadowy operatives who were watching Mr. Montfort. But with all my strength of my being, I was trying to deny that the government of my country could be involved in such base dealings as murder. In any case, I feared that Mycroft Holmes's recommendation to put the affair out of my mind was a vain and futile wish.

I slept only fitfully that night and awoke the next morning with the puzzling affair still lying uneasy in my mind. I was pleased to see that the rain had stopped, though it remained shiveringly cold as I proceeded to the Telegraph Office on the Strand, where I sent the message to Mr. Montfort, as per Mycroft's instructions.

I had already boarded the omnibus to return home, and was fishing through my bag for the fare, when I came upon the copy of the deed that Ralph Montfort had given me. My first thought was to deliver it to the doorstep of the Diogenes Club and be done with it. I had, however, made a pledge of assistance to Mr. Montfort, upon which it would be rude to renege.

Deciding quickly, I hopped off the omnibus and hailed a hansom to take me to the one place in London where I might actually be able to turn up information regarding the deed, the British Museum.

At the information desk of the Library

I found a tweedy, balding, bespectacled man, whose very paleness screamed of having spent years inside closed rooms in the company of ancient volumes. I requested information on any topical, even trivial events that had taken place during the reign of the second George. After a twenty minute wait, I was led to a table and presented with three huge bound volumes of brittle newspaper sheets, dating back to the early 1700s. I then began the arduous task of weeding through page after page of brittle, yellowed newsprint, scanning the pages for the name of Montfort, without success, as it turned out. I skipped over most of the second volume, until I came to a collection of the London *Gazette*, beginning in July of 1752. I worked my way through to September 12, by now suspecting there was little chance of anything directly relating to the land grant appearing in the newspaper, though now simply curious to see what else had happened on that day.

Imagine my disappointment at coming upon the edition dated Monday, August 28 through Thursday, August 31, and then having it jump to Monday, September 15th, completely omitting the date in question! I went back and turned the pages once more, to make certain I had not missed any, but there was no question that the prior week was absent. Could someone have got to the newspapers before me and torn the page out? Examining the binding, I could detect no trace of a torn page.

My head was beginning to ache from the mustiness, so I sought out my librarian friend and informed him that I was done with the volumes. 'Did you find what you were looking for?' he asked.

'No, I'm afraid not. There is a gap in the records. It jumps from Thursday, August 31st to Monday, September 15th, with — ' I stopped talking, suddenly realizing that something was wrong. In any given succession of months, the period from the 31st to the 15th was a fortnight plus one day. The date on the newspaper should have been Friday, September 15th.

'May I ask what year you were investigating?'

I informed him of the year, and saw a

knowing smile develop on his face. He quickly explained the discrepancy, seeming to savor his knowledge like the taste of a rare spice. As I listened, I felt a strange excitement, as though I had uncovered a lost secret of the ages, although this one was not so much lost as merely forgotten. But then I realized the implication of what the librarian had told me. I had to see Ralph Montfort immediately. Racing out of the museum I hailed the first cab I spotted, instructing the driver to take me to the Sturridge Hotel.

As it turned out, Ralph Montfort was not in, though another face I recognized was. The homely, pockmarked man whom I had seen outside the Diogenes Club was now seated in the lobby, pretending to read a newspaper. Doing my best to hide my face from the man, I scrawled a note for Mr. Montfort, asking him to contact me at once, then scurried out of the lobby.

Having promised Missy, our maid, the evening out, I prepared my own dinner. I was in the midst of cleaning the plates when a knock came at the door. It was Ralph Montfort.

'I got your note and came over immediately,' he said. 'Have you discovered something?'

'Yes, I am afraid I have,' I said. 'Please come in.'

'Is something wrong?'

'I am afraid, Mr. Montfort, that the deed is a forgery. I am sorry.'

His face fell at the news. 'But it was authenticated by a documents expert.'

'Yes, but not by an historian, who would have known that Great Britain adopted the Gregorian calendar on September 2, 1752, and that in order to bring the nation into compliance with the rest of Europe, eleven days were dropped, resulting in Saturday, September 2nd being followed by Sunday, September 14th. So you see, September 12th, 1752, the date recorded on your deed, never actually existed in this country. Surely the King would have known that and not used the date.'

Instead of taking the news with the distress I had expected, Mr. Montfort laughed. 'I should have known better to allow personal vanity to enter into things,' he said.

'I do not understand.'

'September 12th is my birthday. I figured one date was as good as any other. Obviously, I was quite wrong. You have my thanks, Mrs. Watson, for ferreting out a crucial flaw. I will be sure to change it on my final version of the deed.'

'You mean, you . . .'

The man's eyes, once so doe-like and innocent, now turned hard. 'Forged the document myself? Of course. The first version was not very good. It didn't fool old Rowley for a second, but he graciously told me what mistakes I had made with word usage and spelling, even the colour of the ink and the wax seal before I, shall we say, released him from the obligation of informing the authorities about my plan.' Infinitely more disturbing than Ralph Montfort's shocking revelation was the fact that he was beginning to remove his necktie!

'But the letter he sent to the Prime Minister authenticated the document,' I said, trying not to panic as Montfort took another step towards me, his necktie now taut in his hands.

'I forged that, too, on a piece of Rowley's stationery. The problem was, after I had posted the letter to the P.M., I became concerned that there were other flaws in the document that would brand it a forgery. That was why I decided to consult London's greatest intellect, Sherlock Holmes. I knew if the deed survived his examination, it was ready to present to the government. If, however, flaws remained, Holmes would surely have pointed them out, as you did so accommodatingly.'

'At which time you would have killed him, too?'

'I cannot afford to be exposed, Mrs. Watson, surely you can understand that.' He stepped ever closer, forcing me to retreat, a position I do not favor.

'But what is the purpose of this horrible plot?' I cried.

'Money,' he replied. 'What other purpose is there? I have amassed considerable debts and I am in desperate need of money. Once the palace is convinced that this document is genuine, they will pay any amount to obtain it. I will be a rich man indeed.'

'Is that really worth two human lives, including your own brother?' I implored.

'I have no brother. That was part of the cock-and-bull story I devised to entice Holmes into taking my case.'

At that moment I realized my earlier judgment about Ralph Montfort had been wrong. He was, undoubtedly, the most diabolically skillful liar I had ever encountered. As he continued to advance on me, I subtly shifted my direction towards John's desk, praying that he had left his old service revolver in the middle drawer.

'I know this must seem an ungrateful way to repay you for your assistance,' he was saying, 'but I really have no choice. No choice at all.' He lunged for me and tried to wrap the necktie around my throat, but I anticipated and dodged him, and dove for the desk.

Pulling the second drawer completely out, I found John's revolver amidst the scatter of pens and pipes. With trembling hand, I pointed it at Montfort, shut my eyes and pulled the trigger, but only heard a sharp, metallic *click*.

Then I remembered that I had asked John months ago to remove the bullets while the revolver was stored inside our house!

I cried out as Montfort pushed me into a corner, his repulsive body pressing into me as he forced me against the wall, forced the strip of cloth to my neck. I struck back as best I could, but was no match for his strength. I had all but given up hope when I heard a dull *thud*, followed by groan, and the figure of Ralph Montfort slumped to the floor, unconscious. Behind him stood the mysterious, pock-scarred man who had been following me. Tightly gripped in his hand was a short, heavy club, vulgarly known as a 'life preserver.'

'Are you all right, ma'am?' he asked.

'I . . . I think so. Who are you?'

'My name is Wainwright, I'm a private detective. This man owes my client a great deal of money, and we've been keeping an eye on him, so he doesn't try to disappear without paying up. I followed him here tonight and heard the commotion from outside. Would you like me to summon the police for you?'

'Yes, please,' I moaned, staggering to a chair, and silently vowing that I would never spend another night alone, even if it meant accompanying my husband to the provinces, to America, or to the very gates of Perdition itself.

The Adventure of
the Nefarious Nephew

Although he was quite slender, Sir Peter Swindon, KC, managed to puff out his chest like a pigeon while strutting like a popinjay, his white periwig standing in for a bird's natural crest. I have no doubt that this posturing was impressing some within the courtroom, though I felt it bordered on the comical.

'Now then, Dr. Watson,' he said, absently brushing his moustache with the edge of his monocle, 'you were engaged by Scotland Yard to examine the body of Humphrey Jafford, were you not?'

'I was,' my husband answered from the witness stand.

'And what did your examination reveal?'

From one coat pocket John withdrew a small notebook, and from the other, a pair of spectacles that he had only recently been required to obtain. Using the detailed and technical terminology of the medical profession, he went on to describe the gruesome fact that Mr. Jafford had died as the result of a severe blow to the head from a heavy object. 'Judging from the position of the body and the direction of the blood flow from the wound,' he added, 'it seems clear that Mr. Jafford was facing his attacker, and fell backwards upon receiving the blow.'

'Facing his attacker,' Sir Peter mused. 'And why should he not face his attacker, since he knew him so well.' This statement was pointedly directed towards the defendant, Owen Jafford, the victim's nephew. Strikingly handsome, if somewhat dandified, Owen Jafford was marked by one curious fluke of nature: despite his youth, his hair, which was worn on the longish side, was almost totally white.

But if the prosecutor's objective was to rattle the defendant with his accusation he failed, as young Jafford merely looked away in bored fashion.

'Is it possible, Dr. Watson,' Sir Peter went on, 'that a heavy, silver-headed walking stick, much like the one the defendant carries, could have been the object that was used to kill Humphrey Jafford?'

'It is possible, yes.'

'I see. Was there anything else that you observed while examining the deceased?'

'Yes. The placement of the wound, on the right side of the head, indicated that his assailant was a left-handed man.' I looked back at the now-frowning defendant and noticed that he was indeed holding his walking stick with his left hand. 'And then there was the matter of his closed fist,' John offered.

'Pray, explain yourself, doctor,' Sir Peter said.

'The late Mr. Jafford's left hand was tightly clenched, a muscle contraction that does not occur naturally in death. It occurred to me that he might have been grasping something in his hand at the time of his death, so I asked Inspector Laurie to pry the man's hand open.'

'And what did the inspector find?'

'Hairs,' John said. 'White hairs.'

Sir Peter turned to glare once more at Owen Jafford. 'White hairs found in the hand of a man who had been killed by a left-handed assailant; the evidence speaks clearly for itself, m'lud,' he announced. 'I put it to the court that, having been informed of his dying uncle's intentions to disinherit him, Owen Jafford took it upon himself to speed along his uncle's appointment with the angels before any new will could be drawn up. The two argued, may even have struggled, ergo the hairs in Humphrey Jafford's clenched hand. The encounter rushed to a deadly conclusion when Owen Jafford raised his stick — ' and here the prosecutor thrust his hand dramatically in the air — 'and struck!'

The spectators in the court chamber collectively gasped at the theatrics.

'Thank you, Dr. Watson,' Sir Peter concluded and returned to his table.

It was now time for Mr. Strang, the counsel for the defence, to strike back at John's damaging testimony, which, I feared, was in for a severe raking. I was therefore quite surprised when the opposing barrister calmly announced: 'May it please the court, m'lud, I have no questions for this witness.'

'Indeed, Mr. Strang?' remarked the grim-faced Judge Wilkins, who seemed quite surprised himself. 'Very well, Dr. Watson, you may step down.'

John did so, striding to the back of the courtroom to take a seat beside me. I squeezed his hand in support of a job well done. While I knew John had offered expert testimony in many cases in the past, I had never before seen him in this environment.

In fact, this was my first experience with the criminal court system of Great Britain. I would not have been here at all were it not for my desire to be near John at all times during this break in his successful lecture tour.

Mr. Strang then announced: 'I would like to summon to the stand Lady Emmaline Belgrave,' and the confused reaction of Sir Peter indicated that he knew nothing of this surprise witness.

A small, elegant woman of middle years, clad in a fine crushed velvet dress the colour of berries, made her way to the stand. Mr. Strang bumbled along behind her, revealing a natural Pickwickian sort of dignity that stood in contrast to the affected theatrical pomposity of his opponent.

'Now then, Lady Emmaline,' he began, 'you have heard it stated that Humphrey Jafford met his untimely death on the evening of January the twelfth, 1904, sometime between eight o'clock, when his servant delivered a brandy to him in his library, and half-past eleven, when the same servant checked upon him.'

'Oh, yes, indeed,' she chirped.

'And at that time, Lady Emmaline, where were you?'

'I was at the Royal Opera House in Covent Garden.'

'Were you alone?'

'Quite.'

'While you were there, did you see anyone who is perhaps in this courtroom?'

'Oh, yes,' she said, smiling, 'I saw that young gentleman over there, Mr. Jafford.'

A loud rumble of murmurs now broke out within the courtroom, prompting the judge to call for order. When it had been restored, Mr. Strang continued.

'How long were you at the opera, Lady Emmaline?' he asked.

'Curtain rings up exactly at eight, so I must have been there from about half-past seven,' she replied. 'I like to sit in my box and watch the comings and goings of the other patrons. Since it was Wagner night, the curtain did not ring down until nearly midnight.'

'And Owen Jafford was there the entire time?'

'Oh, yes, the entire time.'

'So there is no way he could have been in Earl's Court on that evening, murdering his uncle.'

The witness shuddered. 'How dreadful, even to contemplate.'

'Thank you, Lady Emmaline,' the portly barrister said, returning to his seat. John, meanwhile, leaned over to me and whispered into my ear: 'There's a development for you!'

It was abundantly clear, however, that Sir Peter was not about to take this development peacefully. He virtually leapt to his feet and approached the stand. 'Lady Emmaline, prior to the evening

101

when you say you saw the defendant at the opera, had you ever met him before?'

'Oh, no,' she replied.

'Indeed? How was it, then, that you came to notice, and keep under surveillance for nearly four hours, a man of whom you had no prior knowledge?'

'As I said, I like to watch people from my box. It so happens that I have been looking for a walking stick to get as a gift for my husband, Lord Belgrave. When I noticed Mr. Jafford take his seat, I said to myself: 'That young man is carrying the exact walking stick I have been looking for.' I made it a point to seek him out after the opera to ask him from whence he had obtained it. I fear the other patrons must have thought me the victim of a robbery, for I ran after him calling, 'Young man, please stop!''

A titter of gentle laughter ruffled the crowd at this. Sir Peter, however, seemed not amused. 'M'lud,' he said, 'in light of this unexpected testimony, I beg the court time to re-evaluate our case.' I noticed a smugly satisfied smile on the face of Mr. Strang.

'Very well,' Judge Wilkins ruled, 'we shall reconvene at ten o'clock tomorrow.' As Sir Peter walked back to his chair, I noticed that he faltered slightly, and for a moment I thought it might be more theatrics, but the concerned expression on John's face convinced me otherwise. Within seconds we were at his side.

'Has the pain returned?' John asked.

'Only slightly,' Sir Peter responded, though his ashen face told a more serious tale.

'I insist on giving you a thorough examination,' my husband said. 'Chest pains are not to be ignored.'

'Accompany me to my office, then, for I have no time to follow you to yours.'

Even though the walk from the Old Bailey to the Inner Temple was an easy one, John decided that a coach ride would be best for the ailing barrister. Once within the Temple, I waited in a clerk-filled antechamber while John conducted his examination in Sir Peter's private office, after which I was allowed inside.

'I have warned you, Sir Peter, against the continued strain of too many cases in succession,' my husband was saying. 'After this one it is imperative that you rest.'

'After I forfeit this one, you mean,' he said gloomily, all traces of the former popinjay having disappeared.

'The defendant does appear to have a strong alibi,' I stated.

'That woman was lying, Mrs. Watson,' he replied, 'The evidence against Jafford is simply too strong, as Strang must have realized, which is why he has miraculously produced an eyewitness at the eleventh hour to put him in a different place altogether.'

'Please, Sir Peter, you must not excite yourself,' John cautioned.

'But can't you see that the young scoundrel is going to get away with it?' the barrister cried. 'I have until tomorrow morning to try and break this alibi, or the case is lost.'

'Perhaps you could beat Lady Emmaline's statements down on the stand,' John suggested.

'No, no, no, you saw how she charmed everyone in the courtroom. I would come off as a reprehensible bully. The question we should be asking is, why would a woman of her station be lying for a young rotter? She must know him, somehow. If only I could prove that, it would destroy her story. But how am I expected to do it by ten o'clock tomorrow?'

'Well, it will do absolutely no good to work yourself into a froth,' John said. 'I am going to prescribe a sedative for you so that you will at least get a decent night's rest.'

'Dr. Watson, if you could guarantee that you would have the solution to my problem by the time I awaken tomorrow morning, I would gladly ingest anything,' Sir Peter said. 'If not, I must continue to work, through the night if necessary.'

'I accept the challenge,' I blurted out, prompting John to turn and stare at me, open-mouthed. 'Before the clock strikes ten tomorrow, you shall have an answer.'

'But how could you . . . ah, I see,' the barrister said, his eyes darting back and forth between John and me. 'You shall get Sherlock Holmes to work on the problem, eh?'

'If he is available. Right, darling?' I said, watching John's face begin to redden.

'Fair enough,' Sir Peter said, suddenly relaxing. 'Go ahead, Dr. Watson, do your worst.'

John stepped out to talk to one of the law clerks, sending him to the nearest chemist for a powder. After instructing Sir Peter as to its administration, he escorted him to the street and hailed a coach to carry him to his home. Then, and only then, did John speak to me.

'What in heaven's name did you mean by promising to solve his case for him?' he demanded. 'And what is this business of getting Holmes involved! You know perfectly well he is off somewhere on this American crusade of his and cannot even be contacted!'

'John, I did not promise that Mr. Holmes would be involved,' I said. 'I suggested that he may help if he were available, which, as we know, he is not. Nor did I say that we would solve Sir Peter's case. What I said was that we would have an answer for him. The answer may well be: 'Sorry, we cannot help you'.'

John was glaring at me now, and doing a rather good impersonation of a smouldering log in a fireplace.

'Oh, don't look at me that way, dear,' I protested. 'You saw the state the poor man was in. This was the only way he would have agreed to your prescription.'

John sighed. 'Yes, you may be right. Still, I don't like to see him get his hopes up only to be dashed.'

'Then we must do whatever we can to see that his hopes are not dashed,' I replied.

Since John had to return to his surgery that afternoon (rather than atrophy as a result of his recent absence, his practice had seemed to grow), he headed off in one direction and I another. I arrived home, chilled from the brisk January weather, to find Missy, our maid, dusting the bookshelf. 'Thank you, dear, for cleaning this off for me,' I said, pulling down the Debrett's that we had somehow acquired, yet rarely used.

I quickly found the entry for Lord Hugh Belgrave, but discovered it to be less than revealing, being largely concerned with his lineage. It did, however, confirm that his lordship had taken a wife named Emmaline, a union which produced a son named Richard. I read the entry over and over, looking for some kind of clue, which, of course, was not there. Then, as Missy continued her chores, I sat back and tried to imagine what Sherlock Holmes would do in this situation, given the scanty facts. The answer came quickly.

I snatched up yesterday's edition of the *Times* and turned to the theatre listings. A cry of delight escaped my lips (which rather startled poor Missy) as I read the schedule for the Royal Opera House.

When John arrived home several hours later, he was surprised to find me in evening wear. 'Where are we going?' he asked.

'To the opera, John,' I replied. 'It's Wagner night.'

A light, but not altogether unpleasant, snow salted our clothing us as we stood in queue at the box office of the opera house. Our seats were not particularly good, though to be honest I have never been much of an enthusiast for Wagner, favouring less portentous music. But witnessing the performance was only a secondary reason for my presence. After searching virtually the entire house bottom-to-top, I finally spotted Lady Emmaline, in an upper loge box, seated next to a young man. I kept my attention focused on her throughout most of the first act, and at the first interval, watched as she and her companion exited through the back. Quickly rising from my seat, I started to slide past John.

'Where are you going in such a hurry?' he asked.

'I must not lose Lady Emmaline,' I responded.

'I am coming with you,' he said, rising himself.

'No, she might recognize you from the trial. I must do this alone.' Leaving him, I made my way up the aisle and entered the crowded foyer, where the chances of finding one person in particular seemed impossible.

Being rather tall, however, I was able to peer over the heads of most of the multitude. Before long I spotted Lady

Emmaline Belgrave standing at the bar next to her young companion, who was sipping a brandy. As I fought my way through the throng to get to them, I realized I had but one quick chance to try and obtain the information I was seeking. I also realized that now was not the time for subtleties.

'Lady Emmaline, isn't it?' I called, as soon as I was within earshot, and the woman turned to me.

'Yes?'

'I thought so,' I said, wedging myself next to her. 'Perhaps you don't remember me, but we met through a mutual friend, Owen Jafford.'

But before she could reply, her young companion spun around and faced me. 'Do we know you, madam?' he demanded.

'Dickie,' she scolded, 'don't be so dreadfully rude.'

'I am sorry,' I went on, 'I was just telling Lady Emmaline that we have a mutual friend, Owen Jafford — '

Dickie Belgrave's darkly handsome face melted into a black scowl. 'Never heard of the blighter,' he said sharply, 'and I will

110

thank you, madam, to mind your own business. Come along mother, let's go back.' She was still protesting as the young brute pulled her through the crowd towards the stairs.

It was obvious to me that the name Owen Jafford meant something to Dickie Belgrave, something he chose not to acknowledge.

I quickly returned to John, who was chatting amiably with another patron. 'Darling, let's go,' I said, excitedly.

'But we have only seen one act,' he replied.

'Please, John,' I entreated.

'Oh, very well.' Excusing himself from his previous conversation, he accompanied me to the coat room.

In the freezing cab on the way home, I told him of my encounter with Lady Emmaline; though, to my surprise, he failed to share my excitement.

'That was a rather foolhardy thing to do, Amelia,' he uttered. 'You tipped them off to your game.'

'There was no time to do anything else,' I protested. 'But if Sir Peter put

Dickie Belgrave on the stand — '

'Belgrave would deny knowing Jafford, just like as he denied it to you,' John said. 'And being the son of a peer, he would be believed.'

Then taking my icicle hand in his, he added gently: 'I am sorry, Amelia, but the law requires proof, not merely intuition. It may be true that Lady Emmaline and her son are both lying, but how can you prove it? Ah, here we are.' The cab pulled to a stop in front of our home.

Spending the time required to prepare for bed in silent rumination, I had to accept the fact that he was right. We had failed. More precisely, I had failed, and Owen Jafford was soon to be a free man.

'Aren't you coming to bed?' John asked.

'I think I will stay up for a bit and read,' I said. 'Maybe it will drive away this horrid sense of frustration.' From the shelf I selected Mr. Dickens's *Christmas Books*, which I had been meaning to re-read since the yuletide, and turned to my favourite among these tales, *A Christmas Carol*. I savoured the familiar prose until my eyes began to tire and droop, and with growing effort I read the description of the second midnight spirit:

Its hair, which hung about its neck and down its back, was white as if with age; and yet the face had not a wrinkle on it, and the tenderest bloom was on the skin.

Whether I had actually dropped off into sleep or not, I do not know. All I can recall is suddenly sitting up, vividly awake, a light beam having been switched on in my mind. I had found the flaw in Lady Emmaline Belgrave's testimony!

Being of generous nature, I let John sleep rather than rushing into the bedroom and waking him up with the news, though I myself tossed and turned excitedly throughout the night. Early the next morning, however, we were en route to the home of Sir Peter Swindon to tell him of my realization. His initial reaction was all that I had hoped for.

'That is brilliant, Mrs. Watson!' he cried, but then ruined it by adding: 'If only you were a man, you would make a splendid lawyer.' Why, oh why is it that so many men would just as soon accept the existence of Mr. Wells's Martian invaders than believe that a woman is born with a brain? I opened my mouth to respond to him, but before I could, he let out a gasp and clutched his chest, then slowly sank down to one knee.

'Sir Peter!' John cried, rushing to him and helping him off the floor to a nearby couch.

'This is the worst one yet,' gasped the lawyer.

'We must get you to the hospital immediately,' John declared.

'But the case . . . ' Sir Peter croaked.

'The case is not worth risking your life over,' John replied, sternly. The judge will simply have to delay the proceedings until you are well.'

A sardonic smile rose through the fear and pain on the lawyer's face. 'Strang would not let that go unchallenged,' he uttered. 'He is holding all the cards at present, and would protest that this was nothing more than a confusion tactic. He would badger Wilkins for a dismissal, and likely get it.'

As I watched and listened helplessly, an idea began to form in my mind, one that was so audacious, so riotous, that I tried to push it out, but it would not go. 'Perhaps I can help,' I offered. 'What if I were to question Lady Emmaline in court?'

'You?'

'Yes, along with a few visual aids such as . . . well, might I borrow a suit of yours, Sir Peter?'

'A suit?' he queried. 'You mean you wish to appear before the Bench posing as me?'

I wanted to tell him that I was simply attempting to meet his own criteria for legal acceptability — namely, being of the male sex — but I fought the urge down. Instead I said: 'I know it probably sounds insane — '

'Because it is insane,' John interjected. 'You must forgive my wife, Sir Peter. She was an actress in her youth and sometimes forgets that all the world is not a stage.'

I was about to rebuff John's comment when I noticed that Sir Peter was regarding me with renewed interest. Through the pain, I thought I detected a shining curiosity in his eyes. Playing up to this interest, I said: 'This may be the only chance to bring Mr. Jafford to justice.'

'Do you think you could do it?' he asked.

'No,' John returned, 'I positively forbid — '

'Yes,' I answered firmly, ignoring my husband. 'I watched you yesterday in court, observed your manner and stance. As we are roughly the same height, it would be a matter of removing my cosmetics, fixing my hair, fashioning a moustache and lowering my voice. And I have experience, of course — I once understudied the role of Portia.'

'I know why you are doing this, Amelia,' John said conspiratorially, 'and I assure you, you do not have to prove anything to either of us.'

'Whatever do you mean, darling?' I asked, innocently.

'Amelia, we are talking about the

King's Bench!' John suddenly cried. 'The Old Bailey is not a theatre!'

'Don't be too sure, old fellow,' Sir Peter said, ending the argument.

I quickly dressed in an old tweed suit of Sir Peter's and set about duplicating his visage over my own. Letting down my hair, I flattened it as much as possible and hid the excess under the shirt collar. Soot from the chimney turned my auburn tresses black like Sir Peter's, and I carefully trimmed some ends, which I attached under my nose with paste to create a moustache. In his closet I found an old, rather dusty, periwig and an unused monocle. Strutting like a popinjay, I made my entrance into the living room.

'God help us,' John muttered. 'The resemblance is better than I would have predicted, but still, you will never get away with it.'

'People tend to see what they expect to see,' Sir Peter said, adding: 'It just might work.'

It was that quietly-spoken encouragement that carried me all the way to the Old Bailey where, less than an hour later, properly robed and bewigged, I faced an audience consisting of judge, jury and on-lookers (including, I noticed, Dickie Belgrave). I silently prayed, then called Lady Emmaline Belgrave to the stand. Immediately, Judge Wilkins interrupted.

'Counsel for the prosecution does not sound like himself today,' he said, frowning, and for a moment I fought down panic. I recovered well enough to say: 'I fear I am catching cold, m'lud.'

'I see,' he acknowledged, albeit skeptically.

'Lady Emmaline,' I began, 'yesterday you testified that you had never before met, or even seen Owen Jafford prior to the opera.'

'That is true,' she confirmed.

'Where were you when you first noticed him?'

'In my regular box in the loge.'

'And where was he?'

'Down below, on the orchestra level.'

'Quite a distance,' I noted, strutting and fiddling with the monocle, while trying to keep my face down. 'And tell me again what you thought upon seeing Mr. Jafford?'

'I said to myself: 'That young man is carrying the exact walking stick I have been looking for.''

'Ah, yes, and then you told us that you ran after him shouting, 'Young man, please stop'.'

'That is true.'

I took a deep breath. 'I confess, Lady Emmaline, that I do not understand that. Anyone truly seeing Owen Jafford for the first time, especially from the distance of a loge box or from behind, would be excused for assuming that he was an elderly man, since his hair is white. Yet, by your own testimony, you knew him to be a young man, and even used that term to call after him — or so you claim. There is only one way, Lady Emmaline, that you could have assumed that Mr. Jafford was a youth of less than thirty, and that is if you had already been acquainted with him.'

A murmur went through the court-room.

'Well, I . . . I . . . ' she stammered.

'What is the truth, Lady Emmaline?' I demanded. 'How long have you known

Owen Jafford? Long enough to lie on his behalf?'

What followed was chaos. Mr. Strang jumped up and began shouting objections, while at the same time, Lady Emmaline turned to her son and called out, 'What should I say, Dickie?'

Leaping to his feet, Owen Jafford shouted back: 'Say nothing, you senile old cat!'

'How dare you speak that way to my mother, Jaffie!' Dickie shouted back, and within seconds, the august proceeding was a shambles. Through all the shouting, however, I was able to hear Lady Emmaline's excited testimony, which was directed towards the judge. 'They told me it would cause no harm to pretend I saw Jaffie at the opera,' she was saying. 'They said it was the only way Jaffie would be able to get the money he owes my Dickie.'

Judge Wilkins, meanwhile, was pounding his gavel to the breaking point in the attempt to bring about order. Once it had finally been restored, he announced: 'The prisoner at the bar will be remanded into custody until such time as I have had the opportunity to confer with counsel for both sides. I wish to see the prosecutor immediately.' With that he stepped down from the bench and motioned for me to follow.

With considerable trepidation, I followed him to a surprisingly austere chamber located behind the courtroom, which was furnished only with a desk, two chairs, an odd framed painting or two, and an array of filled bookcases. He began to remove his robes and wig, and bid me do the same. The game was over. Slowly, and trembling with fear, I removed the garments and pulled the pasty moustache from my lip.

The judge's gaze turned into a stare, then a gape. 'Good God!' he said. 'I knew you weren't Swindon, but I had no idea you were a woman! Who in blazes are you, and where the devil is the real Swindon?'

Hesitantly, I introduced myself and explained that Sir Peter had suddenly taken ill and was under the care of my husband, emphasizing that John was vehemently opposed to my impersonation. There was no sense in ruining my husband's reputation as well.

'The doctor is a sensible man,' he said.

'I know that, my lord,' I said, softly.

'On the other hand, without this decidedly brazen act of yours, we would never have got the goods on Jafford, would we?'

'You, too, believed him to be guilty?'

'As sin. And quite honestly, were I prosecuting this case, faced with these peculiar circumstances, I might have condoned such extreme measures myself in order to convict the blackguard.'

'Is that why you did not expose me at once?'

He shook his head. 'I did not expose you because I did not want to reduce the courtroom to a circus until I figured out what your game was. But then I became rather interested in your line of questioning.' Having said that, his face became quite stern. 'But I must caution you in the strongest terms not to attempt this again. Given the circumstances, the high regard in which I hold your husband and, frankly, the results, I am willing to overlook this absurd charade. But I will not be so forgiving in the face of any future assaults on the integrity of the Bench. And one more thing: you are not to tell another living soul what you have done here today. Is that clear?'

'Perfectly, my lord, and thank you,' I said, sighing with relief.

The reaction from the excitement in the courtroom was still at such a pitch in the hallways of the Old Bailey that I was able to wedge past an army of reporters and slip out of the building unnoticed. Equally anonymously, I boarded the omnibus that carried me home.

John would demand a complete explanation of course, as would Sir Peter, though aside from them, I anticipated no difficulty in complying with Judge Wilkins's command for silence. For even if I were to tell anyone of my escapade in court, who would believe it?

The Adventure of the Ocean Queen

'This really is a great honour, you know,' my husband said, as we made our way up the promenade of the RMS *Ocean Queen*. 'Being invited to dine at the captain's table is tantamount to a Royal command.'

'I only hope I am up to it,' I moaned, bitterly regretting my choice of lobster remoulade last evening at dinner. John, of course, was not the slightest bit bothered by the food, our cramped quarters, nor the movements of the ship on the open sea.

We were only halfway through an eight-day voyage across the Atlantic, the final leg of John's lecture tour of America, where he had been invited to spread the legend of his singular friend Mr. Sherlock Holmes (and spread it rather thickly, I might add).

With support from my husband, I staggered into the dining salon and to the captain's table. There we introduced ourselves to our fellow dining companions. A small, ferret-faced American businessman named Alfred Pontelli rose to greet us, though his wife Lucinda remained seated (perhaps herself a victim of last evening's lobster). They were joined at the table by a bejewelled American society matron named Ursula Woodruff and a rather taciturn baronet from Salisbury, Sir Reginald Miller. Captain Stanleigh soon appeared, a tall, sturdy man, crisply resplendent in his white nautical dress uniform, whose full, greying beard caused him to resemble His Majesty, King Edward. After greeting everybody, he took his seat at the table.

'Thank you for joining us this evening, Dr. Watson, Mrs. Watson,' he said in a commanding voice. 'I have read with interest your stories detailing your association with Sherlock Holmes.'

'Thank you, sir,' John said, beaming.

Mr. Pontelli's head suddenly sprung up. 'Sherlock Holmes?' he cried. 'You mean you're *the* Dr. Watson? I've read your yarns, too. You know which one I liked the best? The one about the big dog running around Dartmouth.'

'Dartmoor,' John corrected.

'Yeah, wherever. It was great!' Turning to his wife, he said, 'Lucy, this is the guy who wrote that book!'

Lucinda Pontelli did not reply. She merely looked at my husband with a rather unfocused expression, then went back to nursing a glass of wine. 'My wife doesn't read much,' Mr. Pontelli said tensely, then he fell silent, leaving Mrs. Woodruff free to monopolize the conversation for the rest of the meal. In addition to speaking rather shrilly, she gesticulated with such abandon that her diamond bracelets were at risk of sailing off her wrists with every pronouncement.

A good deal of her chatter concerned her late husband, an industrialist with a penchant for philanthropy, who was presently, in her words, 'golfing with the angels.' Sir Reginald, meanwhile, rarely took his eyes off his plate, eating mechanically, appearing lost in some burdensome secret thought.

Dinner continued in this fashion until the final course, at which time the ship's purser, an eager young man named Jeavons, approached the table bearing a folded slip of paper.

'Begging your pardon, sir, but I have a message.'

'Give it here, then,' Captain Stanleigh replied.

'Sir, it is for Mrs. Woodruff. It was left at my station with instructions to deliver immediately. By whom, I don't know.'

'Let me see,' she cried, taking the note and studying it with an expression of frivolous delight. 'Oh my,' she squealed, 'that naughty boy. I am afraid I must leave you now.' Bidding us goodnight, she bustled out of the dining room.

'I wonder what that was all about?' Mr. Pontelli asked, as the wine steward reappeared to refill his wife's glass (for the fifth time, by my count).

'A summons, I should think,' said Sir Reginald, practically the first words he had spoken. 'I cheated a look at the note and was able to read, 'I must see you at once.' It then it went on to say something about lifeboats. I didn't catch it all, actually.' His haunted eyes dropped back down to his plate.

'An assignation?' Mr. Pontelli said, with a leer. 'Who would have thought the old girl had it in her?' And while I confess to having had a similarly uncharitable thought, I would not have expressed it in so base a fashion.

The waiter appeared a moment later to remove my dessert cup, which I had left untouched. 'Are you sure you have had enough to eat, Amelia?' John asked.

'Quite,' I replied.

'I've had enough, too,' Mrs. Pontelli stated, standing with some difficulty, leaving her husband to mutter: 'I'll drink to that.'

'And I am afraid I must return to the bridge,' the captain said, rising. 'May I walk you to your stateroom first, madam?' he asked the noticeably tipsy Mrs. Pontelli. With a crooked smile, she accepted the captain's arm and the two strode away.

'At least him I trust,' Mr. Pontelli said, his eyes following them, 'anyone else I'd half expect to find in my stateroom when I got back.' Then turning to my husband, he said: 'Hey, Doc, would you care to join me for a pipe, a brandy and some cards in the smoking lounge?'

'Indeed I would!' John practically crowed. Then as an afterthought he turned to me. 'Will you be all right on your own this evening, dear?'

'I suppose so,' I said, disappointed, but lacking the heart to deprive him of an audience with one of his readers. 'I am feeling better. I may take a brief walk, get some air, then turn in.'

'Do you want to join us, Sir Reginald?' Mr. Pontelli asked.

'No, I am feeling rather tired, I believe I shall retire,' he said, though I sensed that something more than mere fatigue was troubling him.

'Good evening, then,' John said, and after giving me a brief kiss on the cheek, he scurried away with his new friend. Sir Reginald offered me a nodding bow, and likewise left the salon.

Feeling somewhat abandoned, I repaired to the deck. The night was chilly and moist, and I pulled my squirrel wrap tightly around my neck as I stepped out onto the deck. I gazed out into the infinite blackness of the night around me, listening to the lap of the waves and savouring the tranquil spill of moonlight on the dark surface of the water.

The combined effect of darkness, water, moon and stars had an oddly calming effect on me, and I cannot say how long I stood there, mesmerized. All I can say is that at some point the tranquillity was shattered by a shrill scream.

From behind me a voice cried for help, and two officers appeared seemingly out of nowhere and ran towards the sound. Curious, I followed them across the dimly lit deck of the ship. On the other side — port or starboard, I haven't a clue — near a lifeboat station, a small crowd was beginning to form around the prone body of a woman. As I neared, I saw that the crying figure on the deck was Mrs. Woodruff!

'Let me through, please,' one of the officers shouted, and the group parted before him. 'Are you hurt, madam?'

'No,' Mrs. Woodruff panted, 'but my jewels! My beautiful, precious jewels! That horrible man took them!'

'What man?' the officer asked.

'I don't know,' she replied. 'He came up behind me, struck me down and then robbed me!'

The officer turned and addressed the gathering. 'Was anyone present a witness to this crime?' he asked. No one stepped forward. 'In that case I must ask you to disperse. This is a matter for the captain.'

Reluctantly, the curious passengers began to drift away as the officer helped her to her feet. I, however, rushed forward. 'May I be of any assistance, Mrs. Woodruff?' I asked.

She squinted in my direction for a moment, then said: 'Oh, it's you, dear. Yes, perhaps you could assist me back to my stateroom.'

'And who are you, ma'am?' the officer asked me.

After explaining my connection with the matron, the officer allowed me to take charge of her while he sent for the captain to inform him of the crime. Once the crewmen had gone, I took the woman's arm and said: 'Where is your stateroom, Mrs. Woodruff?'

'Oh, never mind the stateroom,' she cried. 'I need something to help me recover from his horrible ordeal!'

'Something' consisted of three gins from the ship's bar, where, unable to resist taking advantage of her loquacious nature, I asked her to recount her ordeal in detail. 'I was supposed to meet a friend by the lifeboats and while I was waiting for him to arrive, a man came up behind me and demanded my jewels.'

'How did he know you were wearing jewels?' I interrupted.

'He saw them earlier, I suppose,' she replied. 'Jewellery is for displaying, not hiding. I've never made a secret of mine.'

'Could you identify this man?'

'He was just a shape with a coat and a hat that was pulled down over his features,' she said. 'I could see nothing of his face. But I smelled something.'

'Oh?'

She leaned closer to me. 'Whisky,' she said. 'The man had been drinking whisky. I smelled on his breath when he demanded my jewels, and when I refused, he shoved me to the deck and tore them from my wrists, then fled.'

At that moment the officer who had responded to Mrs. Woodruff's cry for help rushed towards us. 'There you are, madam. The captain has been looking for you.' He rushed back out again and returned shortly with Captain Stanleigh, for whose benefit Mrs. Woodruff repeated her story.

When she had finished, the captain said: 'May I ask, madam, who sent you the note you received during dinner?'

'You may ask, but I shan't tell you,' Mrs. Woodruff replied, coquettishly. 'It is a personal affair.'

'That may be, Mrs. Woodruff, but it also seems likely that the man who sent you the note was the same man who assaulted and robbed you.'

'Nonsense,' she declared. 'He would never harm me.'

'Yet he failed to keep his appointment with you, leaving you the target of a thief.'

'He had an excellent reason for not announcing his presence,' Mrs. Woodruff declared. 'We must be very discreet when we are together. To say any more would be indelicate. I am sure when he arrived, he saw that I was at the centre of a commotion and decided to move on.'

'Very well, Mrs. Woodruff,' the captain said, 'we will talk further tomorrow. For now, get some rest. Walters, take Mrs. Woodruff to her stateroom and see to anything that she might need.' Snapping a salute, the young officer took the matron's arm and escorted her out. When they had gone, the captain turned to me and said: 'Mrs. Watson, would it be possible to consult with your husband about this nasty business?'

'I am sure he would be thrilled,' I replied. 'When last seen he was heading to the smoking lounge with Mr. Pontelli.'

'Let us go then,' he said, and at once we were off on a labyrinthine inner-deck journey to the smoking lounge. Upon entering the lounge, the captain received the automatic attention of everyone therein — everyone except my husband, who was absently cleaning out the bowl of his pipe. The captain strode over to him and had a word while I surveyed the smoky interior of the room. Mr. Pontelli, who had invited John here in the first place, was nowhere to be seen.

Responding to the captain's summons, John quickly took his leave. When we were out on the deck, heading back to our stateroom, I mentioned that I had not seen Mr. Pontelli.

'Yes, curious, that,' John said. 'After one quick round of all-fours he got up and left, said he had to check in on his wife. He never came back. He even left his whisky sitting there.'

'His whisky? I thought you were having brandy,' I said.

'Whisky better suited the surroundings. But do not worry, dear, I had only one.'

We soon arrived at our tiny stateroom, which was one deck below the dining salon. 'This is your room?' the captain said. 'Surely we can do better than this for such a distinguished guest. We shall move you to better quarters first thing in the morning.'

'That is very good of you,' John said.

'It's the least we can do in return for your assistance.' After informing John of the robbery, Captain Stanleigh's expression turned grim. 'I must now ask you not to repeat what I am going to say to anyone else. This evening's robbery was not the first such since we left New York Harbour. There have been three other reports of missing jewellery. Each time the article in question was discovered missing from a stateroom. Tonight's was the first actual assault. We have kept things quiet, naturally, so as not to worry or frighten the other passengers.'

'How does the thief get into the staterooms?' I asked.

'We have no idea. There is never a sign of forced entry.'

'Isn't there a safe on board for people to place their valuables?' John queried.

'Of course. Watching over the safe is the responsibility of Jeavons, the purser. But we can only recommend that passengers lock their valuables up, we cannot demand so.'

'It sounds like the thief could be anyone on board,' John said. 'We have virtually no information with which to start an investigation.'

'On the contrary, dear, there is one little clue,' I said. 'Mrs. Woodruff told me that her assailant smelled of whisky. When exactly did Mr. Pontelli leave the smoking lounge, John?'

'Oh, really, you can't possibly think that he — '

'I know how distressing it must be to consider one of your readers a suspect, darling, but it is our only clue.'

'Very well,' John said, 'he left no more than ten minutes after we arrived in the lounge.'

'And if I had to guess,' I went on, 'I would say it was roughly fifteen minutes from the time the two of you left the dining salon until I heard Mrs. Woodruff scream, so it is possible.'

'If only we knew who sent that note,' the captain mused.

'Perhaps the note itself contains a clue to the identity of the sender,' said John.

'Possibly, but if the woman refuses to name its sender, I doubt she would turn over the note. She may even have destroyed it by now.'

'Sir Reginald saw it,' I interjected. 'If questioned, he might be able to remember more of its contents than he mentioned at dinner.'

'An interesting thought,' the captain said. 'Unfortunately, I have no time to play the role of detective. Might I be able to persuade you, Dr. Watson, to carry out a discreet investigation on my behalf?'

'I will be more than happy to help, of course,' John said, and I was gratified to hear him add: 'As will Amelia.'

'Very good,' Captain Stanleigh said, stepping to the door. 'I will send Jeavons around first thing tomorrow morning. He can give you the number of Sir Reginald's stateroom and see to your move to larger quarters.' After a brisk 'good night,' he left us.

As he was dressing for bed, John said, 'You don't seriously think that Pontelli is mixed up in this, do you?'

'He seems to have had the opportunity,' I replied. 'Then again, so did Sir Reginald.'

'Or the captain, for that matter, if opportunity is our only criteria.'

I crawled into the small, short bed. 'I keep thinking about Mrs. Woodruff's coy comments regarding this secret friend of hers. They must be discreet, she said. Why?'

'Obviously because the man is married.'

'Which brings us back to Mr. Pontelli.'

'Or any one of what must be a hundred married men on board,' he said, likewise slipping into bed.

He was right, of course. 'I can see that this problem is going to keep me awake all night,' I moaned.

Fortunately, that prediction proved to be wrong, and I awoke the next morning feeling more refreshed that at any time during the voyage.

After a quick breakfast in the dining salon, John set out to find the missing (or at least misplaced) Alfred Pontelli and get his story of the previous night. I returned to our stateroom, where I was met by young Jeavons, the ship's purser.

'The captain sent me 'round about your stateroom transfer,' he said. 'Sorry I'm a bit late, but I was delayed taking care of a problem.'

'Nothing serious, I hope,' I said, opening the door to our room.

'Rather,' he replied. 'My stateroom passkey seems to have gone missing.'

'Really,' I mused. That would certainly explain how the thief entered the staterooms. 'How long has it been missing?'

'I only noticed it gone this morning, but I haven't had need of it since we left New York, so it may have been missing for days without my realizing it.'

'Could it have been stolen?'

'I hadn't thought of that. It's possible, I suppose, providing the thief knew where to look for it. But that's even worse than losing it.'

'Does the captain know about this?'

'Not yet. I was hoping I would find it and not have to bother him. Speaking of the captain, he asked me to give this to Dr. Watson.' He handed me a slip of paper on which was written the name *R. Miller* and the number *143*.

'I will see that he gets it,' I said, adding that we would be ready to move to our new stateroom by early afternoon.

Since John was otherwise engaged, I set out to find stateroom number 143 myself. After locating it on the upper passenger deck, I knocked on the door and was nearly pulled inside by the force of its opening. A tense Sir Reginald Miller stood in the doorway. After a moment, he recognized me and relaxed somewhat. 'Oh, forgive me,' he said, 'I thought you might be the ship's telegrapher.'

'No, I had a question,' I said, 'but if this is a bad time — '

He shook his head. 'Please come in.'

If this was the kind of stateroom John and I were to move into, I would be quite content for the rest of the voyage. It was spacious and airy, with a living room area separate from the bedroom. Off in the other room I noticed what appeared to be an odd shrine on the man's dresser. At its centre was a framed photograph, next to which was a folded cloth bearing a Star of David, the symbol of the Jewish faith. Glancing around, I could also not help but notice an open bottle of whisky resting on a table. Even at this early hour, Sir Reginald had been drinking.

'I would not disturb you, Sir Reginald, but there has been a bit of trouble involving Mrs. Woodruff, which may have something to do with the note she was handed at dinner. The note that you saw.'

'Oh? I am afraid I saw very little of that note, actually. Only what I reported at the time. Sorry.'

'Oh, well, thank you anyway. I'm sorry to have disturbed you. Good day.'

'No day on board this ship is a good day,' he snapped.

'Seasickness?' I asked.

He shook his head. 'I do not wish to burden you, Mrs. Watson, but I feel as though I must talk to someone before I go mad! Can you stay a moment? Please sit down.'

He went into the bedroom and retrieved the photograph from the dresser and handed it to me. It showed a boy, perhaps twelve years of age. 'My son and heir, Benjamin,' he said. 'I was visiting America when I received word that he had been severely injured in a riding accident. I was advised to return home immediately. I booked passage at once.

Every day I ask the ship's telegrapher to try and signal for news, but it never arrives. Every day I pray to God to keep my son alive until I return. The days at sea, trapped on this ship, powerless to do anything . . . ' He poured another whisky for himself.

What could I say? I attempted to comfort the poor man as best I could, with a total lack of success, and then excused myself, leaving him to his agony and sorrow.

I returned to the stateroom to begin packing and was shortly joined by John. I relayed what I had learned from the purser as well as the tragic story told by Sir Reginald, who in my opinion was guilty of nothing except fatherly love.

'We can also dismiss Pontelli as a suspect,' John said. 'He really had gone back to his stateroom to check in on his wife, not because he was concerned about her delicate condition, but because he was convinced she was being unfaithful to him and he hoped to catch her in the act. He even brought a witness, who I have also questioned. As it turned out, his suspicions were unfounded, and Mrs. Pontelli was merely asleep. But Pontelli's whereabouts up to the time of the assault on Mrs. Woodruff can be accounted for.'

'So the primary suspect now is Mrs. Woodruff's secret friend, but we have no idea who that is.'

'I wish Holmes were here to put this right,' John sighed.

'Incredible as it may sound, darling, so do I,' I replied.

The move to our new, indeed luxurious stateroom was accomplished swiftly and we sought out Captain Stanleigh to thank him and offer our report, such as it was. After that, I confess that my thoughts turned more to poor Sir Reginald than to Mrs. Woodruff. In fact, I hardly thought of her at all until dinner that evening, when she burst forth upon our table, beaming, and grandly displaying her stolen jewellery!

'The captain said you two helped in the investigation, so I wanted to thank you personally,' she cried.

'Where were your jewels found?' John asked.

'In the stateroom of Sir Reginald Miller,' she declared. 'Can you believe it?'

'Frankly, no,' I said, shocked.

'Oh, I'm afraid it's quite true, dear,' she said. 'I encountered Sir Reginald on the promenade this afternoon. He was acting quite peculiarly. I approached him to say hello, and immediately smelled whisky on his breath. Well! I ran to the captain as fast as I was able, I demanded an immediate search of his stateroom. There, in a dresser drawer, I'm told, they found my jewels!'

'I simply can't believe it,' I muttered.

'It took me back as well at first,' she said, 'but you know, you can't really trust his kind.'

'His kind?' John asked.

She glanced from side to side as though fearful of being overheard, then said, 'The Jews.'

Fortunately for Mrs. Woodruff, I am a lady, and was therefore prevented from saying to her what I was thinking. Instead through gritted teeth I asked, 'Where is Sir Reginald now?'

'In the ship's gaol, where he belongs. They are still looking for other missing pieces. Apparently, I was not his only victim. Well, good evening to you both.'

She walked away, perhaps having sensed my displeasure with her presence.

'Well,' was John's only comment.

'I cannot accept this,' I told him. 'The man I saw this morning was no more capable of assault and robbery than am I.'

'Perhaps you were taken in by a clever performance.'

'No, there is more yet to this tale.'

'Perhaps,' my husband said. 'One thing is certain, though: if Mrs. Woodruff does not stop waving her diamonds under people's noses, someone will try to steal them again.'

'No doubt, but jewellery is made for displaying,' I said, mocking the woman's piping, American voice, 'and not hiding.'

'From the sound of it, she would rather hide Jewry than jewellery,' John muttered.

'Good heavens, darling, you've just made a joke!' I said.

'Have I?'

'Of course, when you said that . . . oh!' My hand instinctively went to my forehead.

'What is it, Amelia?'

'Oh, good heavens, now things make

sense! You were right, John, I was taken in by a clever performance. We must find the captain at once!'

That was not a difficult task, since he was seated at his customary dinner table, with a new array of guests for this meal. We managed to convince the captain to abandon his dinner and repair to his quarters, where I outlined my suspicions.

Within a half-hour's time, all of the parties whose presence I had requested had joined us. The gathering included Sir Reginald, Mrs. Woodruff, Jeavons, and three officers. And even though he could not readily be seen, I knew that there was one other present. For her part, Mrs. Woodruff was greatly disturbed by the unshackled presence of Sir Reginald, but Captain Stanleigh quieted the gathering and then allowed me to take the stage, as it were.

'I believe we can settle the issue of the shipboard robberies from this very room,' I began, 'but I would first like to ask a few brief questions. Mr. Jeavons: did Mrs. Woodruff visit you at the purser's station at any time during the voyage?'

'Yes, on the first day,' he replied. 'She came down to inspect the safe, but decided against locking up her jewellery.'

'Thank you,' I said. 'Now, Sir Reginald, did you at any time invite Mrs. Woodruff into your stateroom?'

'Of course not,' he replied, 'why would I?'

'Well, you invited me in,' I reminded him.

'Yes, but . . . the answer is no, I did not invite this woman into my stateroom.'

'And even if he had, I would not have gone!' Mrs. Woodruff huffed.

'I will accept that,' I said, looking past her and seeing the figure that had just stepped out from behind a door. 'Mrs. Woodruff, behind you!'

'What?' she said, spinning around. Directly behind her was a figure in a long coat and slouch hat, which was pulled down to obscure his face.

'Who on earth is this?' she asked impatiently.

'Doesn't that man look familiar?' I prodded. 'Is he not dressed exactly the way you described your assailant?'

'What? Oh, yes!' she cried. 'Yes, it's

him! Wait, it can't be him! It was Sir Reginald who robbed me!'

'Thank you,' I said to the cloaked figure, who removed his hat and coat and revealed himself as Alfred Pontelli.

'Anytime,' he said, grinning.

'What sort of game is this?' Mrs. Woodruff demanded.

'A game to prove that Sir Reginald was not the man who robbed you, Mrs. Woodruff. Neither was Mr. Pontelli. Neither was it your secret friend, because that man does not exist. You invented him for our benefit. Furthermore, by failing to recognize the very figure you described, you have confirmed my suspicion that you never saw any assailant, because there never *was* an assault. In fact, Mrs. Woodruff, you were never robbed!'

'That's absurd!' she cried.

'It was you who stole the passkey from the purser's station,' I continued. 'You robbed the other passengers, then staged your own robbery, including sending yourself the note, to throw suspicion onto someone else. The note, which you had delivered to yourself, was part of the ruse.

To make your story more realistic, you added the detail of smelling whisky on the man's breath, and I am sure you rejoiced this afternoon when you detected liquor on the person of Sir Reginald and found your perfect suspect, someone who was already acting strangely, not out of guilt, but rather out of worry over his injured son. So you waited for him to leave his stateroom, then hid your jewellery in there for the captain to find.'

'You are insane, I never set foot in that stateroom!'

'No? Earlier this evening you made a comment disparaging Sir Reginald's faith, did you not?'

'What of it?'

'How, Mrs. Woodruff, did you know Sir Reginald was Jewish?'

'What a silly question,' she replied. 'Who else would possess a Star of — ' She stopped suddenly.

'A Star of David,' I finished for her, 'a symbol of faith which I noticed in Sir Reginald's stateroom, but which he does not display in public, like jewellery. You could only have known about it if you had been inside his stateroom.'

The woman appeared to deflate before our eyes. She slowly started to sink and the captain rushed forward to catch her and ease her into a chair, where she sat with one shaking hand covering her eyes. 'How careless of me,' she uttered. 'It is my husband who is to blame for this. When he died, he cruelly cut me out of his will. After all those years with him, he left his fortune to charities where it would be eaten up by the under classes. They had no right to that money! Those people were used to being poor I was not! It's not fair. Not fair at all.'

'Take her back to her stateroom and keep her under 24-hour guard until we dock,' the captain told one of the officers. 'Search her room, and get that passkey from her.' Then turning to Sir Reginald, he offered his hand. 'I cannot apologise enough, sir, for the indignity to which we have subjected you. If there is anything I can do for you, please name it.'

'Can you establish contact with the mainland? I must know of my son's condition.

'It shall be a priority,' Captain Stanleigh said, commanding one of the young officers to escort Sir Reginald to the wireless room.

John and I repaired to the ship's bar for celebratory champagne, then back to our new stateroom for another restful evening. The next morning we encountered Sir Reginald at breakfast, although it was a completely different Sir Reginald who greeted us. Smiling and happy, he rushed over to shake John's hand and kiss mine.

'We received word this morning, Benjamin is out of danger,' he reported. 'My son is recovering.'

Later that day, we happened to spot the Pontellis standing on the deck, looking out at the sea, arm in arm like young lovers, whatever marital troubles had passed between them seemingly blown away.

'Perhaps it is the sea air,' I said to John, nudging him back towards our spacious, private stateroom.

The Adventure of the Burnt Man

I am not certain which was the more disturbing: the dream I was having in which my husband John turned into his peculiar friend, Mr. Sherlock Holmes, at a most inappropriate moment, or the bloodcurdling scream that shocked me out of it.

I was the first to leap out of the bed, followed a second later by John, who muttered: 'What in heaven's name was that?'

Another scream was heard, and it appeared to be coming from our sitting room! While I donned my gown, John retrieved his old service revolver from a drawer in the wardrobe and called out, 'I am coming out and I am armed!' To me he hissed: 'Stay in here, Amelia.'

'Help me!' a voice cried, and I immediately recognized it as that of our maid, Missy.

'We are coming!' I called back, ignoring John's order to remain behind. We stumbled into the dark sitting room together to find the poor girl on the floor, fighting hysteria.

'What is it?' John demanded.

'Oh, sir, tell me he's gone!' Missy implored.

'Who's gone?' I asked, switching on the electric light and squinting under the sudden flood of light. There were times when I longed for the days of gaslight, when you could control the brightness of a room by adjusting the intensity of the flame. But it was 1904, and progress could not be stopped. While I occupied myself with blinding the three of us, John poured a whisky for Missy and held it up to the girl's lips. Unused to liquor, she spluttered and nearly choked, but at least she regained control.

'Now, Missy,' John said, setting the glass down, 'tell us what frightened you.'

'A man,' she said, in quivering voice, 'a burnt man. Here in the sitting room.'

'A burnt man?' he repeated.

'All black he was, and smelling of

charcoal and ashes,' Missy went on. 'He shoved me down and growled at me, and then he disappeared.'

John and I glanced at each other. 'Are you sure you weren't dreaming?' I asked.

'No ma'am, I saw him.'

There seemed to be a chill in the room, and I noticed that the fire had gone out. I dashed back to our bedroom to fetch my spare robe, which I draped around Missy. Eventually she was calm enough that we were able to transfer her from the floor to the chaise, where she asked for another sip of the whisky. 'Do not develop the taste for that my dear,' I admonished her, 'you are far too young.'

'Start again from the beginning,' John said, handing her the glass, despite my frown.

'Well, sir,' she began, 'I was lying in my bed, tossing and turning, unable to sleep, and I thought I heard noises coming from the sitting room. I listened for a minute, but they didn't go away. So I came out to see what the noises were and that's when I saw the man. Burnt to the bone he was. It was horrible! I screamed, and he rushed toward me and pushed me down. He snarled at me and showed his teeth and they were like a skull's teeth, but a couple were missing. And then he put his boots on and . . . and that was the last I saw of him.'

While I stayed with Missy, John examined the door to our rooms, and found it to be securely locked from the inside. Then he examined each window, and found the same. Even if someone had got into our home, there was no way he could have gotten out again.

'But I saw him!' Missy cried.

'I know you believe you saw something,' I said, soothingly, 'but really, dear, couldn't it have been a dream? I mean, the business of this intruder stopping to put on his boots is exactly the sort of illogical detail that remains from a vividly-remembered dream.'

'Just so,' John agreed.

'But I did see him!' Missy cried again, leaping up and striking a rather petulant pose, as my robe fell from her shoulders. 'Why won't you believe me?'

'There, there,' I said, trying to comfort

her, 'it is not a question of believing you, it is merely a question of . . . oh, dear.' The blood in my veins suddenly froze as I looked at Missy's plain cloth nightdress. 'John, come and look at this,' I said, directing his gaze to her right shoulder.

'Great Scott!' John uttered as he examined the black, ashy handprint on her plain nightdress, evidence that someone had indeed pushed the poor girl to the floor. 'It seems we owe you an apology, Missy,' my husband acknowledged, 'though what I cannot understand is how the man escaped? And what did he want here in the first place?' A look of alarm arose upon John's face and he cried, 'Good Lord, my bag!' then bolted into the small room he uses as a study. He returned a moment later with his medical bag, the contents of which he was examining.

'The underground trade for opiates is on the rise,' he said, 'as are reports of burglaries at hospitals and surgeries. Yet nothing appears to be missing, thank heaven. Missy's scream may have thwarted his attempt, forcing him to flee.'

'But flee where?' I asked. 'What's more,

how could he have got in?'

The clock in John's study chimed three times. 'I am afraid I do not know,' he said, through a yawn. 'I shall have a clearer head in the morning. Perhaps the answer will come then.'

After John had prepared a mild sedative for Missy, the three of us retreated to our respective beds. As I lay there, wishing that John had likewise prepared a draught for me, I muttered, 'Darling, what do you suppose this business of the boots is about?'

'Wanted to be quiet, I imagine,' he mumbled, and in less than a minute, I heard his familiar, low snoring.

Things had returned to normal by the next morning, save for Missy's mood, which resembled that of a frightened heroine from a three-volume novel. When I could take no more of her twittering, I sent her out to Covent Garden to purchase some flowers in the hope that the fresh air might do her good.

John, in the meantime, had searched every inch of our home, looking for any trace of Missy's 'burnt man,' but found none. 'I am afraid we have fallen victim to the girl's overactive imagination,' he declared.

'How then do you explain the hand-print on her shoulder?' I countered.

'I believe I can answer that,' John replied, sounding positively *Holmesian*. 'I am of the opinion that Missy made it herself. Think about it for a moment. Given the peculiarities of her description of the man, and the seeming impossibility of an actual break-in, I must conclude that it was a dream after all. So let us speculate that Missy was sleepwalking while having a horrible dream about an intruder. She walks toward the hearth, trips, falls against the fireplace, catches herself but gets soot on her hand, wipes her hand on her gown, making the print, then begins to wake up. The smell of the ash and soot registers in her dreaming mind as a burnt figure. She screams, then tries to run, falls, and that is how we find her.'

'Did you notice traces of soot on her hands?' I asked.

'No, but neither was I looking for

them,' John replied.

'The handprint, though, was on her shoulder, not the place one would automatically wipe one's hand.'

'Reverse the order of the scenario. She screams, runs, loses her balance or trips, falls and strikes the floor with her shoulder, and instinctive puts a hand to the sore spot. What do you think?'

'I think we should take another look at that nightdress in the light of day.'

We wasted no time entering Missy's small sleeping quarters. I did not want her to return home and find us there, since I have always prided myself on allowing the girl her moments of privacy.

'There, on the wash-stand,' I said, spotting the nightdress. Rushing to it, I picked it up and felt dampness on the shoulder where the stain had been. She had scrubbed it out in the wash basin. 'Oh, Missy,' I moaned, 'why do you pick the most inopportune times to be neat and thorough?'

'That's that,' John muttered. 'I therefore rest upon my deduction, since it is the only explanation possible. And you know what Holmes always said.'

'Yes, yes, when you eliminate the impossible, the remaining explanation, no matter how improbable, must be the right one.'

'I am glad it is settled,' John said, taking up his medical bag and placing his new hat smartly on his head. 'I am already late for my surgery.'

I was alone for some time after John left, since Missy was taking longer than usual for her errand, though when she returned with a breathtaking bouquet of fire-coloured tulips, I had to applaud her judgment.

'Sorry, ma'am, if I'm a little late,' she said, 'but there was a man in the Garden passing out handbills for a carnival what's come to town.'

'A carnival *that's* come to town, Missy,' I corrected, taking the handbill from her and examining it. It promised the usual fare of animals, midgets, thin men, bearded women, mentalists, and something called 'The Insect Boy,' the prospect for which made me shudder. 'If you ask me, dear, sideshows are the ghastliest

161

form of entertainment in existence, unfit for civilized society.'

'I also stopped at Smith's when I saw this displayed,' she went on, holding out the new issue of *The Strand Magazine* upon which was emblazoned: '*The Problem at Braxton Grange,*' *a new Sherlock Holmes story*. 'I know the doctor likes to keep extra copies. I hope I did all right.'

'I am sure he will appreciate your thoughtfulness, Missy,' I told her, laying the magazine down on his work desk, blissfully unaware of the magnitude of problem that *The Problem at Braxton Grange* was about to become.

I spent the rest of the morning quizzing Missy about the singular (to use John's favorite word) episode of the previous night, and had managed by the afternoon to convince her that she had indeed dreamt the entire thing. Her acceptance that it was a nightmare brought her a visible relief, which I shared. But no sooner had the air of normality been returned to our home than John burst through the door, too early by hours, clutching something in his fist and shouting: 'Have you seen this?'

He threw down on the table a copy of the same magazine that Missy had purchased.

'Oddly enough, I have,' I answered. 'I take it by your manner that something is amiss?'

'Amiss?' John cried, reddened to an alarming hue. 'Piracy is what it is, modern day piracy!'

The forcefulness with which John spoke sent Missy scuttling to her room and no doubt undid the entire morning's lesson in calm rationality. 'John, what on earth is the matter?' I asked

'I did not write this story, Amelia, that is the matter! Someone has written a story using my name and *The Strand* actually published it without checking with me first! I am going to telephone them this instant and give them a piece of my mind!'

As he angrily shouted for the exchange operator, I opened the magazine and began to peruse the story. It was certainly written in John's style, so much so that I would not have been able to judge it a forgery. I could not help but wonder if he had at last become so overwhelmed by the personality of Sherlock Holmes that he was now writing stories in his sleep. Behind me, John was shouting something into the telephone, then of a sudden his voice quieted.

'You've received what?' he said, hollowly. 'I will be right down.' He slammed the phone down and rushed to his desk.

'What is it now, dear?' I asked

'It seems the entire world has gone mad, Amelia. George Fortescue at *The Strand* told me they have actually received a letter from some blighter charging that he is the true author of my stories, and that I have written nary a one! Can you imagine?' He marched to his work desk and began rifling through a lower drawer.

'How dreadful,' I commiserated. 'What are you looking for?'

'The journal containing my notes of all the cases I have been on with Holmes. All I have to do is show George my notes and have him compare them with the finished stories, and the claim made by this man, whoever he is, falls to pieces. Blast, where did I put it?' He pulled open another drawer and began to search through it. 'And what is this?' he asked, wiping some black substance off the tops of some papers. The more he searched the more frantic he became. 'I know the journal was in here!'

At once I was at his side, helping him to examine the open drawers of the desk. 'Look here, John, and here,' I said, pointing out more of the black residue.

'What is it?'

'Ash and soot. There are traces of it in every drawer and your journal is missing.' I felt suddenly chilled. 'He was here, John, Missy's burnt man really was here. He must have searched through your desk and stolen your journal. I know it sounds insane, but what other explanation fits the evidence?'

'And without my journal . . . blast!'

I had a hard time keeping up with John as he raced down to the street and hired a cab. He was uncharacteristically silent as we made our way to the offices of *The Strand Magazine*, where a very tall, nearly hairless man greeted us at the door. John introduced him to me as

George Fortescue, and the man ushered us in and led us to a private office.

'We received this letter this morning, Dr. Watson,' Mr. Fortescue said, handing him a single page covered with neat handwriting. John read aloud: 'I feel that the time has come to notify you, the publishers of the Sherlock Holmes stories, purportedly written by Dr. John H. Watson . . . *purportedly* written?'

'Read on, John,' Mr. Fortescue entreated.

' . . . were in fact composed in their entirety by myself, with no help from Dr. Watson, save for the use of his original notes, which he supplied to me in the form of a journal.'

John lowered the letter and muttered, 'Oh, dear God,' before continuing to read: 'Since I have received no monetary compensation for my work, as was stipulated in my original agreement with Dr. Watson, I am appealing directly to you. It is my hope that we will be able to resolve this matter as gentlemen, without the necessity of my lodging a suit in the courts. I shall remain in touch. Yours, Dan A. Coloney. Oh, really!' John tossed the letter back to

Mr. Fortescue. 'I have never heard of this Coloney in my life. This is extortion, pure and simple.'

'And it must be related to the theft of your journal,' I stated.

'Theft?' Mr. Fortescue asked, looking confused.

'Yes, it appears someone broke into my home, though I cannot begin to tell you how, stole the very journal that this blackguard speaks of in his letter, and then disappeared into thin air. And Amelia is right, the timing between the theft and this letter is too close to be a coincidence. I should like to question this Mr. Coloney.'

'Unfortunately, there was no address on the envelope,' Mr. Fortescue said. 'I have no way of contacting him. Though if what you say is true, there is nothing to worry about. Even if this fellow does file a suit he will eventually be exposed as a villain. Try to bear in mind the good news, John: *Braxton Grange* has pushed the current issue to new sales levels.'

John's eyes flared. 'Yes, about that story, George,' he said, tensely, 'I did not write it. It was probably scrawled by this Coloney blighter.'

Mr. Fortescue glared at my husband then passed a hand over his head, as though in remembrance of hair. 'Now you are confusing me. First you vehemently deny that someone else has written your tales, then you say that *The Problem of Braxton Grange* is not your work. Really, John, do you think me a complete fool?'

My husband looked shocked. 'Of course not, George. Why would you even say that?

'Do you not think that after all this time I know your handwriting?' Mr. Fortescue opened a desk drawer and from it pulled out a manuscript, which he threw across the desk to John. As John examined it, his mouth fell open. Then he passed it over to me. I was indeed John's handwriting. 'If you elect to refuse the £100 I was about to send you for the story, John, that is your business entirely. But as you can see for yourself, I have acted honourably.'

'I . . . I do not understand,' John stammered, appearing dazed, and while I did not understand either, I felt nothing but sympathy for my husband, whose distress was obviously genuine.

'Please excuse my husband, Mr. Fortescue,' I said, gently lifting John to his feet. 'He has had a difficult day. Thank you for your time.'

I led John out of the offices and set about hailing a cab myself. On the way home John muttered, 'Nothing makes sense anymore, Amelia. It is like everything has been turned upside-down. I feel like I have fallen down the rabbit hole.'

'I know, darling,' I said, soothingly. 'But there has to be some kind of rational explanation for . . . oh!' I held a hand to my forehead.

'What?' John said, snapping out of his daze. 'You've figured something out, haven't you?'

'Down the rabbit hole, of course! John, tell the driver to go faster, we must get home as soon as possible.'

The hansom driver complied and within minutes we were back on Queen Anne Street.

'At least tell me what you have figured

out,' John begged, as we dashed up the steps and entered our house.

'There!' I cried, pointing triumphantly to the fireplace in the sitting room. 'That is how the man got in and that is how he escaped. He descended through the chimney.'

'You must be joking, Amelia,' John said. 'The shaft opening is far too narrow. Don't you remember how much trouble that chimney sweep had last winter?'

'But John, it has to be the answer,' I protested. 'It fits perfectly with Missy's description of a burnt man. The thief wasn't burnt, he was covered with chimney soot. He left sooty handprint on her nightdress and traces of soot in the drawers he searched through.'

'We had a fire that night, Amelia, he couldn't have got past that.'

'No, darling, I remember feeling a draft and noticing that the fire had gone out. The man no doubt extinguished the embers himself, from above.'

'But if someone really had come down the chimney like some demented Father Christmas, wouldn't he have also left black footprints?' John argued.

'Not if he took off his boots and left them on the hearth,' I said, excitedly. 'Missy specifically stated that the man stopped to don his boots before disappearing!'

Missy herself had now emerged from our bedroom, feather duster in hand, to see what the commotion was about.

'Still, Amelia, the problem of how a grown man could fit through the chimney seems insurmountable,' John said.

'Perhaps it wasn't a grown man,' I replied. 'Perhaps it was a child. Or perhaps . . . Missy, do you still have that handbill advertising the carnival?'

'In my room, ma'am,' she said, then left to get it.

'Carnival,' John muttered, 'those things seem to be popping up everywhere. There was one set up in at least half of the cities in which I lectured last year. I even joked that the carnival appeared to be following me.'

'Indeed?' I said. 'And while you were informing the public about your adventures with Mr. Holmes, did you ever mention your journal?'

'Oh, I'm sure I must have at some . . . Great Scott!'

Missy now returned with the handbill and gave it to me. 'Look at this, darling,' I said, pointing out the words: *Professor Pinky, the World's Smallest Man*. 'That, I daresay, is our burnt man.'

'Extraordinary!' John cried.

'All I have done, John, is eliminate the impossible and reveal the truth, however improbable,' I replied, and I must confess that I was beaming as a result of my deduction. It took only a second, though, for Missy to undermine my entire argument.

'I'm sorry, ma'am, but it wasn't like that,' she said. 'It wasn't a teeny tiny man. The burnt man was a tall 'un.'

'Tall,' I muttered.

'Yes'm. Tall and nothing but bones.'

I glanced again at the handbill and at once realized where I had made my mistake. I beamed once more.

'Missy, dear,' I said, 'how would you like to accompany us for an outing this evening?'

172

Ordinarily when we go out, John enjoys dressing in his finest evening wear, and I enjoy it as well, since he cuts a remarkably dashing figure in a tie and tails. But for this evening I encouraged him to don his country suit and his oldest hat, while I similarly dressed down, lest we be victimized by every pickpocket and swindler in London. Missy had somewhat less difficulty achieving a working class appearance.

We set out by cab for the carnival, which had set up on the green of Archbishop's Park, near the notorious Bethlehem Hospital, and the din of the wretched sideshow greeted us even before we had fully crossed Lambeth Bridge. The cab came to a halt in front of a crowd of people, all waiting to enter the tented area.

'Oh, isn't it wonderful, ma'am?' cried Missy, the poor dear. I made a mental note to take her to the theatre so that she might discover refined entertainment. After waiting in line an interminably long time, we paid our money and were allowed in.

'I want to see the human pincushion!' Missy squealed, but I reminded her that we were there for a purpose. We struggled through the crowd (and really, didn't these people have anything better to do?) until we came to a tent over which was spread a banner reading: '*Nature's Mistakes.*'

'Exploiting unfortunates like this, it is unconscionable,' John muttered, and I fully agreed. However, as I have stated, we were there for a purpose.

Plunging into the dark, stale-smelling tent, we hurried past Professor Pinky (who while small, hardly lived up to the showman's boast as World's Smallest Man) and the Insect Boy, who turned out to be a lad who either ate or pretended to eat insects.

At last we came upon the object of our search, a pitiful specimen of humanity who called himself Pete the Skeleton, the World's Thinnest Man. In this case, the claim was not an exaggeration. The man was horribly wasted, with the bones literally showing through his pale skin. Upon taking a deep breath for the crowd, his spine was visible through his stomach.

Yet for his lack of flesh, he did not appear to be sickly or frail. Rather, he proved his strength by lifting weights!

As Missy stared at the ghastly creature, entranced, I whispered to her: 'Is that your burnt man?'

'He's bony enough,' she replied, 'but he's not burnt.'

'The illusion that he was burnt was the result of soot from the chimney, or perhaps blacking used for disguise. But is it he?'

As she was deliberating, another woman in the crowd shouted: 'I can't take it anymore, I have to leave!' and dashed away from the exhibit. This amused the living skeleton, who broadly grinned, revealing a smile bereft of several teeth.

'That's him!' Missy shouted. 'I remember those missing teeth! That's the man what pushed me down!'

I did not even have time to correct her grammar before the Skeleton spotted us and quickly dashed through a curtain behind his platform. John leapt up onto the makeshift stage and disappeared through the back, and after dispatching

Missy to fetch the police, I followed.

The backstage area was dark and smoky, lit only with oil lanterns, but we were able to make out Pete the Skeleton talking with a short, bulky boulder of a man.

'Mr. Coloney, I presume?' I said, and the short man glared at me, demanding, 'Who are you?' Then he saw John.

'You I know,' he muttered, and a moment later his rough face blanched. 'Crikey, you're Dr. Watson!'

'That's right,' John said, advancing on the man, 'and I do not take kindly to thieves. You have something of mine, and I want it back.'

'You're barmy,' Coloney said. 'I don't know what you're talking about.'

'I'm in no mood for games,' John uttered, putting his hand into his jacket pocket, where I knew his service revolver lie. I prayed he would not draw it unless forced to. 'The fact that you recognized me proves your duplicity. I remember this carnival in several of the cities I toured with my lecture on Sherlock Holmes. No doubt you attended at least one of them and heard me speak of my journal, the source for all my stories. So you used this poor creature to break into my home, steal my journal, and then try to extort money from my publisher by claiming to be the real author of my stories. Do you deny this?'

'I don't have to say anything to you,' Coloney answered, defiantly.

'Perhaps you would care to wait for the police, instead,' I said. Then I saw John's hand grasping the revolver inside his coat pocket. Unfortunately, the Skeleton saw it, too.

'He's goin' for a gun!' the Skeleton shouted in a remarkably deep voice, and before John could withdraw the weapon, Coloney grabbed one of the oil lanterns and threw it at him. Only by pitching headlong to the ground was John able to dodge the burning projectile, which crashed against the rear wall of the tent. Coloney reached for another lantern but was prevented from grasping it by John's bullet, fired from the ground, which penetrated the villain's forearm. With a cry, Coloney clutched his arm and sank to his knees, but now an even sharper cry came from the Skeleton: 'Fire!'

Looking behind us I saw the broken lantern surrounded by a pool of fire at the base of the canvas wall.

'The whole place'll go up!' the Skeleton cried.

'Get him out of here,' John commanded, pointing to the injured Coloney. 'Amelia, go out and evacuate the tent. I'll try to put out the blaze.'

'No, John!' I cried.

'Amelia, *go*!' he commanded, taking off his coat and using it to beat out the flames.

The three of us — one wretched, injured extortionist, one ghastly living skeleton and myself — dashed through the curtain and onto the stage, and I was relieved to find that now less than a half-dozen people inside the exhibit. As I ordered them out, I was equally relieved to see Missy reenter with two constables in tow.

'Fire, backstage!' I shouted, and one of the officers raced back to help John, while the other dealt with Coloney, who, it turned out, had only suffered a superficial wound. John and the officer emerged shortly to announce that the flames had been extinguished.

After telling our tale to the officers, they took Coloney and the Skeleton into custody, and we were allowed to return home.

It was days before John was notified that his journal had indeed been recovered (in addition to a catalogue of items from previous burglaries), though it would remain police evidence until the trial of the two thieves. I thought the news would relieve his black mood, but I was quite mistaken.

'What is the matter, John?' I demanded, growing weary of his sulk. 'You have helped the police solve a case and you have ensured the return of your journal. Why are you in such a mood?'

'That blasted story,' he replied, '*The Problem of Braxton Grange*. If Coloney did not write it, and it appears he did not, then who did?'

'I have been thinking about that,' I told him. 'There is only one person familiar enough with both your style and your handwriting to have forged the story. Furthermore, that person would be eminently qualified to write about the exploits of Sherlock Holmes.'

'Oh, good heavens, Amelia, you can't mean that Holmes himself wrote the story and sent it to *The Strand*?'

'Darling,' I purred, 'haven't you heard that whenever you eliminate the impossible, the remaining explanation, no matter how improbable, is the correct one?'

Try as he might, John was unable to stifle a chuckle.

The Riddle of
the Young Protestor

'Ma'am, a coach has stopped outside, and a man is getting out,' our maid Missy announced, as she peered through the curtains of the front window. Coaches — as opposed to hansoms, growlers, or those new motorized, double-decked monstrosities — are somewhat rare in our street, which is a respectable, but hardly opulent, neighborhood of northwest London.

'He's coming to the door!' Missy cried, excitedly.

Her excitement having fuelled my own curiosity, I stepped to the window to watch with her. Of the man in question, I could see nothing, though stopped at the curb was a stylish, deep green phaeton, drawn by two magnificent horses, which were kept in rein by a stern-looking, high-hatted driver.

I was not expecting anyone this

morning, and if the visitor was looking for my husband, Dr. John H. Watson, he was destined for disappointment. John was off on another of his lecture tours, this one through Scotland. According to his last letter, even the dour Scots were devouring the accounts of his long association with his erratic friend, Sherlock Holmes. John had been taking his increasingly flamboyant tales of his life with the great detective to the masses for nearly six months, and the public's appetite for all things Holmes seemed insatiable. I daresay that the only place in the Empire where the litany of Holmes, Holmes, Holmes, Holmes, Holmes, had worn out its welcome was right here at 17 Queen Anne Street. But I do not intend to spoil a perfectly good day with ruminations about Sherlock Holmes.

A rapid knocking was heard at the door, and Missy sprang away to answer it. I confess that I was equally interested in seeing who our mysterious visitor might be, though I was in no way prepared for the revelation.

Missy led the man into the day room. He was of middle age and diminutive

— barely five feet tall, if even that — and dressed in a fine pearl grey suit with matching gloves and homburg hat. Once the hat was doffed, I could see that his dark hair was oiled and neatly parted in the middle. He regarded me with an air of upper-class superiority that would have carried to the furthest balcony of an opera house.

'This gentleman is here to see you, ma'am,' Missy said, with as much propriety as she could muster.

Once the shock at the man's appearance had subsided, I began to laugh. 'Harry!' I cried.

'Hello, ducks!' he said, a broad, lopsided grin spreading over his elfin face. 'Never expected to see ol' Harry all toffed up like some bloomin' duke, did you, my girl?'

Harry's sudden transformation from upper-class dandy to Cockney jester left Missy clearly taken aback. I came to her rescue.

'Missy, I know you have heard me speak of my friend, Harry Benbow. More years ago than I care to remember, he and I were on the stage with the Delancey

Amateur Players. Harry was the company comedian, while I was an ingénue. Harry, this is our maid, Missy.'

'Hello, love,' Harry said to her, waggling his eyebrows. 'How about gettin' ol' Harry a cup o' water, my girl? I ain't had a chance to stop for my mornin' pint today, so I've worked up a thirst.'

Missy retired to the kitchen to get the water.

'Sit down, Harry,' I offered.

'Like to, ducks, but I don't have much time,' he said. 'The coachman won't wait forever.'

'I hope you at least have enough time to explain this entrance and that outfit.' The last time I saw Harry he had been in considerably more modest circumstances, and was buskin' for coins in Victoria Station. 'Have you discovered buried treasure?'

'Funny you should say that,' he replied, as Missy returned with the water, which he downed in one gulp, and handed back the glass. 'You are now looking at Havilland Beaumont, esquire, expert in antiques.'

'Is this a joke, Harry?'

'Not a bit of it. See, long 'bout a month ago, I was mindin' my own business, makin' a bob wearin' a sandwich sign for this new coffee shop down in Covent Garden. As I was walkin' around the garden, takin' in the booths and whatnot, I see this table with a set o' old dishes that were dead ringers for the ones my granny used to have. Her proudest possessions, they was. Then I see that this cove is callin' 'em antiques and sellin' 'em for nice prices. First chance I get, I crawl out o' my sign and have a look at 'em, and as I'm lookin' the cove starts givin' me all kinds of rabbit-and-pork about when they were made, who made 'em, and where, only he's got it all wrong. So I start repeatin' what my granny used to tell me about 'em, and before you can say Fanny's yer aunt he starts askin' how 'tis that I know so much about antique plates. So, ducks, what am I supposed to say? That I'm just a bloke whose dear ol' gran learned him about plates, and thank you very much for not callin' the peelers on me, guv? Not on your nellie. So I says, 'Well, sir, I got this twin brother who's a downright expert on antiques' — '

'Oh, Harry, you didn't!' I interrupted.

'I didn't think it would hurt nothing. But then the cove starts humming and hemming, and before you know it, he hands me a card and says to go tell my brother to show up at an antiques shop in Mayfair that's run by a friend o' his. So I leave my sandwich sign right where sits and run over to the Hammersmith Theatre, where the doorman's a mate, and he lets me into the costume room. I walk in there as plain ol' Harry Benbow, and walk out as Havilland Beaumont, esquire.'

As he spoke the last three words, Harry appeared to grow two full inches in height, and his natural Cockney accent disappeared so completely into the proper tones of an upper-class gentleman that he could have fooled a Member of Parliament. Whatever else Harry Benbow might or might not be, he was a first-rate actor.

'I rushed over to the address the cove'd given me,' he went on, 'and next thing I know, I'm bein' taken on as a consultant by the right honourable firm of Edward

Chippenham and Company, dealer in matters antiquarian.' He spoke the last word as if practising its pronunciation. 'I had to return the costume to the theatre, of course, but with all the bees-and-honey they're payin' me just to show up, I went out and got one o' my own!' He raised his arms and spun around, displaying the outfit proudly. 'Matchin' turtles and titfer to boot!' he added, holding up his gloves and hat. 'And I get to use the boss's coach whenever I need to.'

'And so you have come here to preen like a peacock, is that it, Harry?'

'*Gor*, Amelia, I wish it was as simple as that. I don't mind tellin' you I've really put my foot in it this time.'

This was hardly a surprise, since every time I saw Harry, he was in some kind of trouble. 'What have you done now, Harry?'

'Well, everything was goin' swimmin' until this woman came into the shop with this old family document that she wanted to know all about, and Mr. Chippenham himself puts me on the job. Now both of them and her are expecting me to figure this thing out, and I can't make tops-or-tails out of it! Well, I sat down and said to myself, 'Harry, if there's anyone who can dig me out o' this hole, it's your friend Amelia's pal Sherlock Holmes.' So here I am. Let's go see the ol' boy. I can take you in the coach.'

I tried not to bristle. 'Mr. Holmes has moved out of Baker Street and I have no way of contacting him,' I said quickly. 'I'm sorry.'

In strictest terms, that was the truth. Mr. Holmes had indeed left 221B Baker Street not long after John had abdicated his position as the great detective's live-in biographer, preferring to become my husband. It was a move that Mr. Holmes continued to view as an act of desertion. It was equally true that I could not immediately put anyone in contact with Mr. Holmes, though what I was holding back from Harry was that I might have been able to locate him through his brother in White- hall, Mycroft, with whom I had, strangely enough, developed a cordial acquaintance over the past year. But I was still too angry to even consider it.

Neither had I any intention of informing Harry about the incident that had taken place in our home not a week prior, only a day or two after John had left on his tour.

I was returning home from a visit to the lending library, and I knew Missy to be out shopping. Yet when I arrived at our home, I found the front door unlocked! Thinking that perhaps Missy had returned early, or had forgotten something, I threw caution away and strode in.

'Missy?' I called, but she did not answer. Entering our rooms, I noticed the door to John's and my bedroom ajar, and started for it. 'Missy, why are you cleaning today? You are supposed to be — '

The shock I experienced at beholding Mr. Sherlock Holmes, inside my bedroom, gazing into my mirror, bedecked in my best green velveteen dress, is difficult, if not impossible, to communicate. After I emitted a gasp that sounded more like a shriek, Mr. Holmes turned casually toward me. 'Mrs. Watson, how are you?' he asked, calmly.

'Mr. Holmes . . . what . . . how . . . ' I

stammered. 'How did . . . did Missy let you in?

'Your girl was nowhere to be found,' he replied. 'But even if she were here, it would make little difference. I have a key.'

'You have a *what*?' I cried.

He fished through the pocket of his trousers, which had been carelessly thrown across our bed and withdrew a key, which he held up. 'The good Watson gave it to me, and offered me use of your home whenever I needed it.'

Oh, this was too much! I would definitely be having words with John about this. But my thoughts were immediately wrenched away by the sound of seams ripping. 'My dress!' I cried. 'Why . . . ?'

'You know that my work sometimes necessitates a disguise, and occasionally, expedience dictates that the most effective disguise is that of a woman,' he said, once more looking into the glass and adjusting the shoulders of the dress. 'I can hardly be expected to walk into to the nearest *couturier* and try on the new Paris fashions. Fortune has it that the combination of your tallness and my leanness means that garments made for you are destined to likewise fit me, particularly if I crouch.'

'But couldn't you at least ask *me* first?'

'If time were not of the essence, I would not have come here in this way. I beg of you to step out of the room, Mrs. Watson, for I must change back into my regular clothes, and your continued presence will do nothing but ensure that you become more knowledgeable about my private physical characteristics than any member of your sex outside of my mother.'

My jaw dropped and I fear my face flushed, and I was unable to utter a word. Silently, though inwardly seething, I stepped into the day room, slamming the bedroom door behind me.

I was still angrily pacing when Mr. Holmes emerged a few minutes later, my good dress wrapped about his arm like a rag, and without so much as a nod, headed for the door. 'This is *intolerable!*' I shouted, trotting behind him.

Stopping, he turned to face me. The excitement that flared in his piercing grey eyes warred with his expression of grim determination. 'So, madam, is a crime without a solution,' he said, quietly, and left.

I had not seen nor heard from Mr. Holmes since that day, nor did I wish to — except to guarantee the safe return of my velveteen dress. But enough of Sherlock Holmes; I had to deal presently with Harry Benbow.

'*Gor*,' Harry was muttering, dejectedly. His disappointment over losing the counsel of Sherlock Holmes, however, was short-lived. Within seconds, his face broke into a broad smile again. 'That's all right, Amelia,' he said, jauntily, 'who needs Sherlock Holmes anyway. You can help my client instead.'

'Oh, Harry, really.'

'Don't sell yourself short, my girl. If it weren't for you, I might still be singin' myself to sleep each night in the clink, 'cause o' that nasty business with those two little tykes.'

In the previous year, I had managed to help rescue Harry from gaol when he had been accused of kidnapping, but that had been done as a friend. I was not ready to hang a shingle outside announcing myself as a detective for consultation. That, however, did not stop Harry.

'Why, if I didn't know better, I'd say you were Sherlock Holmes's long-lost cousin.'

'*Please*, Harry,' I groaned. 'Having him for an acquaintance is challenge enough. But honestly, I know nothing about antiques.'

'You don't have to know anything about antiques,' he said. 'It's an old document with some kind of poem or nursery rhyme on it. The lady who brought it in calls it a riddle. So it ain't the document that's valuable, it's the words that are on it.'

'The words?'

'Right. An' if I know you, you'll be able to come up with the answer to this riddle faster 'n you can unlock a door lock with a horseshoe nail. Not that I'd know how to do that, o' course.'

'Of course,' I said, with a smile. 'Well, I suppose it would do no harm to look — '

'That's the girl!' he cried, clapping his hands together. 'Now, you just leave everything to me, I'll set the whole thing

193

up, don't you worry about a thing.'

After doing another little dance, he flipped his hat through the air and deftly caught it on his head, and reached for the doorknob. 'Got to go now, ducks.' Then, once more affecting the high-born accent, he added: 'I shall be in touch, my deah,' and disappeared from the room.

Still reeling from the sudden appearance of Harry, I did not realize that Missy had reentered the room until she said: 'You know some of the most interesting people, ma'am.'

'Don't I, though?' I muttered.

She stepped back to the window to watch the coach drive off. 'What did he want?'

'One can never be quite sure where Mr. Benbow is concerned, dear, though I am certain I will find shortly find out.'

I did indeed find out two days later when the phaeton arrived once more in front of our home, and this time the driver knocked on the door and handed Missy a note that read: *Amelia, put on your best jewels and go with the driver. HB.*

'My best jewels?' I wondered aloud. With equal parts of curiosity and foreboding, I retired to my bedroom, emerging a few minutes later, adorned with a string of pearls and matching earrings, I followed the driver outside to the coach and rode to the exact destination I had expected, the Mayfair shop of Edward Chippenham and Co.

Harry greeted me at the door. 'So good of you to come,' he intoned, punctuating his words with a wink. Leading me through the shop, which was heavily populated with staff, but surprisingly barren of actual items for sale, we ended up in a plush, paneled meeting room in the back. There, seated at a long, highly polished table was a pleasant-looking young woman — almost a girl, really — who rose and smiled self-consciously as I entered.

Closing the door behind us, Harry gestured toward the woman and said: 'This is Mrs. Jane Ramsay. Mrs. Ramsay, this is our documents expert, Lady Amelia Pettigrew.'

Lady Amelia Pettigrew? I struggled to keep my mouth from flying open at the news of my admittance into the peerage. It was true that I was born Amelia Pettigrew, and I like believe that I am a lady at all times, but only Harry Benbow could take such simple truths and twist them into such a massive deceit.

'Please do be seated, Lady Pettigrew,' he bid me in his *faux* Mayfair accent.

'Thank you,' I said through clenched teeth, taking a seat opposite the young woman.

'Thank you for agreeing to help me, Lady Pettigrew,' Mrs. Ramsay said. 'Mr. Beaumont told me that you would be able to answer all of my questions. I hope you can.'

'As do I, my dear,' I replied, casting a sidelong glance at Harry.

From a small handbag, Mrs. Ramsay produced what appeared to be a letter-sized piece of vellum, which she laid it on the table in front of me. On it, in fading, archaic letters, was written a most peculiar verse:

In the place where Earl and Queen both neale,

Befor the blesing of St. Andrews cross,
Where Lion meets the Mercer shal reveal
A relick of the young Protestors loss.
Upper Tower
Riseing Dudley
Slopeing King
And Castle do surounde
The time at which the relick maye be
   founde.

'What can you tell me about it?' she asked, eagerly.

'I can tell you that whoever wrote it never saw a copy of Dr. Johnson's dictionary,' I replied. 'Where did this come from?'

'Charles, my husband, refers to this simply as 'the riddle.' Apparently it has been in his family for years and years, handed down from one generation to another for as long as anyone can remember, yet its meaning remains unknown. I am taking something of a chance by bringing it here, but I merely wish to surprise him.'

'Surprise him how?' I asked.

'By finding the solution to the riddle. You see, Charles and I have been married only a short time. He is considerably

197

older than I, and . . . well, he is not the easiest man to live with. But I do so want to please him. In the short time we have been together, I have heard him speak of this riddle with almost a sense of reverence, but he continues to puzzle over its meaning. It is not much of an exaggeration to say that this scrap of parchment is the most important thing in his life. It is my hope that by finding the solution, I will be able to make him happy.'

The poor girl was so young, so innocent, so sincere in her desires, that I had to wonder exactly what kind of marriage it was.

I read over the riddle again. Harry was absolutely right; it did read like a nursery rhyme. A lost verse of Mother Goose, perhaps?

'There is one more thing you should know, Lady Pettigrew,' Mrs. Ramsay went on. 'There is a reason that this rhyme is so important within the family. I know this will sound quite fanciful, but the 'relick' referred to in the verse is thought to be some kind of lost treasure. In fact, it is my belief that Charles views this document as some kind of treasure map.'

I looked up at her, and then over at Harry, whose lips were pursed in a wry smile. 'A treasure map,' I mused. 'That is how your husband described this document to you?'

'Actually, no, not in so many words. The truth is, Lady Pettigrew, Charles has never brought it up directly or spoken of it with me in any context. But I have overheard him talking with Mary, his daughter through his first marriage.'

'And have you spoken directly with her regarding this?'

The woman appeared suddenly discomfited. 'I am afraid that Mary and I have yet to become friends. She is only a couple of years younger than I am, you see, and quite headstrong.'

'I take it that the first Mrs. Ramsay is no longer alive?'

'Of course not. Charles is a strict Catholic, Lady Pettigrew, and as you know, the Church does not countenance divorce. I would not be his wife unless his first wife was dead. Perhaps it is the fact that I am Mary's replacement mother that has erected the barrier between us, I don't know. But I do hope you will be able to advise me, even though I cannot afford to pay you much for your time.'

'Not to worry, Mrs. Ramsay,' Harry interrupted. We work on commission.'

I had to admit that this peculiar rhyme and this tale of hidden treasure had captivated my interest — as I am certain Harry knew it would. I asked if I could keep the vellum and Mrs. Ramsay once more showed signs of discomfort.

'I suppose that would be all right,' she said, 'but Charles does not know that I have taken it. It would hardly be a surprise if he had known, after all. So please, Lady Pettigrew, take care that nothing happens to it. I would not want Charles to be cross.'

My heart went out to the poor girl. How difficult was her situation at home? Perhaps I could say something to make her feel a bit more at ease.

'I shall take every precaution,' I assured her. 'And I hope you will not think me untoward by telling you, this my dear, but I can empathize somewhat with your situation. I am likewise my husband's second wife.'

'Then you must know what it is like,' she blurted out. 'Forgive me, Lady Pettigrew, I don't presume to compare my situation with yours, but do you sometimes feel as though you are living in the shadow of your husband's former wife?'

'There is nothing to forgive, my dear,' I said, 'and yes, I often feel the presence of the one with whom my husband had previously shared his life.' *And occasionally, John also speaks of his first wife, Mary,* I thought, but held my tongue.

The young woman smiled. 'Oh, you have no idea how much better it makes me feel to know that my situation is not unique. Thank you, Lady Pettigrew.' She rose and offered her hand, which I took. Then Harry escorted her out of the room. When he returned, he looked like a child who had just won ownership of a candy shop in a sweepstakes.

'Well, Amelia, what d'you think?'

'Frankly, Harry, I feel slightly criminal presenting myself to the poor girl as something I am not. Lady Pettigrew, indeed!'

'Nonsense, ducks, just look at how much better you made her feel by talkin' to her?'

'I suppose so,' I acknowledged. 'But I have no idea if I can actually help her.' I glanced at the piece of vellum again. 'The only lines that make any kind sense are those in the last part of the verse. The references to Tower, Dudley, King and Castle seem to point to young Lord Dudley, the husband of Lady Jane Grey.'

'Lord and Lady Who?'

'Lady Jane Grey was an unfortunate teenage girl who got caught up in the political and religious machinations of Lord Dudley's father, Northumberland, who was an advisor to Edward the . . . sixth, was it? Yes, the sixth . . . who was himself a mere boy. As a result, Lady Jane was proclaimed Queen of England. This was before the time of Elizabeth, before any woman had actually been crowned as Sovereign, so the idea was still somewhat novel. But the plot fell to pieces when

Bloody Mary, the eldest daughter of Henry the eighth, ascended to the throne. Both Lady Jane and Dudley were arrested as traitors, imprisoned in the Tower of London, and executed.'

Harry looked confused. 'I must've missed that day o' school.'

I smiled. 'This comes not so much from school, Harry, as from my years as a governess. History was always my favorite subject, next to literature. Perhaps one day I shall take you on as a pupil.'

'So, is that it, then? The riddle's about this Dudley Grey bloke?'

'I do not know, Harry. Some of the references seem to fit, but others do not. 'Castle' is clear enough — whatever else the Tower of London may be, it is first and foremost a castle. 'Upper Tower' would seem to refer to the place where the prisoners would have been lodged. And 'Riseing Dudley' is likely the young lord, who nearly rose to the status of prince. It would be logical to assume that 'King' is a reference to Edward the sixth, though why he should be 'Slopeing' is anyone's guess, unless there is an archaic meaning to the word. 'Queen' could signify either Lady Jane or Mary, though 'Earl' is puzzling. It might mean Northumberland, though if memory serves, he was a duke, not an earl. As for the references to 'St. Andrew,' 'Lion' and 'the Mercer,' I'm afraid I haven't a clue.'

'But you'll get it, ducks,' Harry said, giving me a wink. 'I 'ave complete confidence in you.'

I sighed. Harry was perhaps my oldest friend, and I was loath to hurt or disappoint him in any way, but inwardly, I prayed that this latest scheme of his would not lead to trouble.

Harry was able to secure the services of the phaeton to take me back home. Once there, I pulled down from our shelf an old book of English history and began to pour over it, hoping that a clue might leap out from the pages to help identify the references in the riddle. Yet the more I read, the more mysterious the lines became.

One of the phrases that continued to puzzle me was 'the young Protestor,' which implied a figure who was actively fighting against a reigning monarch, perhaps even a usurper. Neither Lord Dudley nor Lady Jane fitted that description, since others attempted the usurpation on their unwitting behalf. The reference to 'Lion' might stand for England itself, though 'the Mercer' made little sense. Could it be a name? I glanced through the index of the book to see if I could find any notable personages named 'Mercer.' I found none, though several entries down I came across a name that sent a bolt of realization through my mind: *Monmouth*.

I quickly turned to the pages indicated and skimmed down the history, augmenting what I already knew about the failed attempt to usurp the throne from James II. In 1685, the Duke of Monmouth, the illegitimate son of Charles II, had staged an uprising against James that was as much a Holy War as a battle over the throne, with James on the one side holding strong Catholic sympathies, while the rebellious Duke championed the Protestant cause. The Monmouth rebellion was quickly quelled and the Duke was tried and executed. This appeared to satisfy the riddle's phrase 'the young Protestors loss' far more than did the story of Lady Jane Grey. The association with Monmouth also gave new significance to the fact that 'Protestors' was capitalized — not only did it mean one who was protesting the reigning monarch's right to the throne, but one who was a *Protestant*. What's more, the reference to 'St. Andrews cross,' which was the symbol of Scotland, could now be seen as representing James II, who was also King of the Scots. But then, what of 'Dudley?' How on earth did he fit into the Monmouth rebellion?

After another hour or so of fruitless research, with little to show for the effort except tired eyes and a headache, I decided to put the riddle to rest for the evening.

The next morning, after dressing and breakfasting, feeling quite refreshed, I picked up the vellum once more and resumed work on it, but quickly came to the same stone wall of confusion. It was becoming clear my best course of action was to seek the assistance of a professional scholar.

After informing Missy that I was going out, I stepped out into a sunny and comfortably temperate autumn day, and embarked on a very pleasant walk past shouting news vendors and pungent fish shops, down to Oxford Street, where I caught the bus and rode it nearly to the impressive doorstep of my destination, the British Museum.

Hurrying inside, along with a throng of other Londoners, I went straight to the reading room, located in the building's enormous rotunda, and looked around until I located a gaunt, white-haired man whose stooped frame and thick spectacles bespoke of a lifetime spent among the volumes. From my previous visits, I knew that he was a member of the library's staff, though I had never discovered his name. He was, however, so much a fixture of the reading room that I would not have been surprised to learn that, instead of retreating to his home at day's end, he nightly shelved himself along with the books.

Edging close to him, I whispered: 'Pardon me, but I need some assistance.'

He slowly turned my way. 'Yes?'

'I need to find some information about Monmouth.'

'Oh, yes, Monmouth,' he said slowly, savoring the words. 'Are you interested in the duke or the street?'

'The duke. I doubt the street would help me.'

'Quite so,' the librarian sniffed. 'Please follow me.'

He led me to one particular shelf, where I saw in nearly a dozen volumes devoted solely to the Duke and his imprint upon history. Almost without looking, he selected two volumes in particular, slid them off the shelf and deposited them in my hands.

'These would be the best from which to begin,' he said.

I groaned inwardly as I glanced at the remaining volumes, knowing that it would take a fortnight to comb each book for clues. But dutifully I carried the first two tomes to the nearest desk, while the librarian disappeared into the maze of shelves.

After an hour's worth of reading, I had gained no more insight than that with which I had walked in, except for the discovery that one of my favorite aromas in life, the delicate but unmistakable scent of printed pages in a book, managed to antagonize my nose when the pages in question were aged and dusty enough. I sneezed and snapped the book shut at the same time. This was futile.

'How are we doing?' a voice behind me asked, and I turned to see that my friend, the librarian, had returned.

'Not well,' I admitted. 'Perhaps I should have asked for the street after all.'

'Hmmp,' he snorted. 'I do not even understand why they would name a street after such a traitor, particularly since it was a perfectly fine street, with a perfectly fine name, before. But this is 1904, the modern era, and having made it this far, we must show our gratitude by changing everything that has got us here, simply for the sake of change. And thus, St. Andrews Street becomes Monmouth Street.'

He looked at me as though awaiting a response, but I could form none. Had I heard correctly?

'I'm sorry, but would you repeat that?'

I finally managed.

'I was merely saying that this new century's determination to rebuild, restore and rename this ancient realm has got — '

'No, no, about the street. What is now Monmouth Street was once called St. Andrew's Street?'

'Indeed.'

'Oh,' I uttered, raising a hand to my head. All this time I had been taking of the phrase *St. Andrews cross* in the riddle to mean a representation of the actual cross upon which the saint had been martyred. But what if was not a religious cross at all? What if it signified one street crossing another? Heavens, could it be that the riddle was literally a written road map that pointed the way to its secret?

'Madam, are you unwell?' the librarian asked.

'What? No, I am fine, thank you,' I quickly replied, 'but would you happen to have a map showing the street when it was called St. Andrews?'

'I am positive we do,' he said. 'We pride ourselves here that, given enough time, we can produce anything.' He disappeared into a back room and returned some ten minutes later, proving himself to be as good as his word.

'Here we are,' he said, holding a folded map of the city of London. 'This is dated a mere forty-five years ago, but it is already a repository of obsolete information. I believe you will find what you are seeking here.'

Carrying the map to a nearby table, he carefully unfolded and examined it, his bony finger poised and hovering over a section in the middle. 'Ah, there we are,' he said, dropping his finger on a particular spot. As I examined it, my heart leapt.

After questioning the librarian some more, and making notes of the details of the map, I headed back home. There I telephoned Harry at the offices of Chippenham and Co.

'I have it!' I shouted into the telephone box, a device I normally loathe, but one that, at times, does prove convenient. 'I've solved the riddle!'

'*Gor* . . . I mean, *my word*, it didn't take you long.'

'Honestly, Harry, it came about as much from chance as anything. But I have it.'

I looked down at the sketch I had made from the map, the one that depicted St. Andrews Street crossing not only Earl and Queen Streets, but also Mercer Street where it met its northwesterly extension, White Lion Street. This series of crossings was completely encased by a diamond made up of Tower Street, which moved upward to Dudley, which in turn rose to King Street, which sloped back down to Castle Street.

'The words of the rhyme were all London street names, Harry, pinpointing the last place anyone would look for wealth. They are the streets leading to and surrounding *Seven Dials.*'

'Seven Dials? *Blimey!*' he cried, then caught himself, presumably for the benefit of anyone else at the offices of Edward Chippenham and Co., who might be within listening range. 'Uh, I mean, do tell, Lady Pettigrew,' he uttered in high English.

I continued describing the clues I had found on the map, still marveling at both the solution to the riddle, and the cleverness of its creator. Seven Dials was the area immediately surrounding the convergence of seven streets into a hub, which at one time had been marked by a tall column bearing six sundial faces. It had originally been an attempt at creating a fashionable neighborhood, but it rapidly fell into disrepair, and eventually became one of the worst and most crime-ridden rookeries the city ever had. Recent attempts to rehabilitate the area had helped, but it was still a place to be avoided after dark.

'The most significant clue of the entire riddle,' I told Harry, 'was the one we completely ignored: the word 'neale,' which I took to be a misspelling of *kneel*. But the man who laid out Seven Dials in the late 1600s was named Thomas *Neale*.'

'And there's been a treasure hidden under the bloomin' place ever since,' he mused. 'All this time and no one ever knew.'

'That gets into the most fascinating part, Harry. According to the librarian at the British Museum, the column was torn down by a mob in the 1770s because of the rumor that a treasure was buried underneath it. It seems probably that the source of that rumor was the riddle, which helps confirm that it is indeed as old as Mrs. Ramsay states.'

'*Gor*,' Harry said again, and this time he did not even bother to correct himself. 'Did they find anything when they toppled it?'

'History says no. What's more, the pieces of the column were later taken to Surrey and reassembled about a hundred years later. If anything had been hidden within the stones themselves, it surely would have been discovered already.'

'So it's just a fairy tale after all?'

'Not necessarily. My friend at the museum also happened to mention that, in addition to the six sundials on top, the seventh dial was a column itself, which cast shadows over the neighboring buildings that served to chart the time of day. And what does the riddle say? That 'the time' at which the relic shall be found would be revealed? I believe that something was buried in Seven Dials, and that it was deliberately placed at a specific 'time,' as reflected by the shadow of the column. If we knew what the precise time was, we might be able to pinpoint the location. It would certainly not be easy, since the column is no longer there, but it could be done through mathematical calculations.'

'Amelia, you're a blinkin' genius!' Harry crowed. 'Mrs. Ramsay is goin' to be flyin' over the moon when she hears this. I'll give her a shout right now! I want you to be the one to give her the news, so I'll let you know when to come. Better yet, I'll send the coach round again. Gor bless you, ducks!'

The line quickly went dead. After replacing the receiver of the wretched device, I once again studied the riddle. There could be little doubt that the solution I had derived was the correct one. The fact that all the names mentioned in the riddle corresponded perfectly with the streets of Seven Dials could not be a coincidence. The timing also made sense. The column had been erected in 1694, a mere nine years after the Monmouth rebellion. Perhaps the 'relick' had been kept in a temporary hiding place during the interim, and then its holders decided to secret it in a more permanent location.

Burying it in Seven Dials must have been a simple matter, given the construction that was taking place in the area at that time. The only lack of foresight on the part of the riddle's composer were the assumptions that the column would remain standing forever and the street names would never change.

It all made such perfect sense. Even Mr. Holmes would have had to agree with that. Why, then, did I feel a tiny note of unease about my deduction, as though there were a serious flaw with the analysis that I could not identify? Perhaps I was simply thinking about it too much.

I resolved to set aside all thoughts of the riddle and picked up a book instead. This escapade of Harry's, while it had been intriguing, had put me grievously behind in my reading.

I had got through less than one chapter of *Our Mutual Friend*, by my favorite author, Mr. Dickens, when the annoying jangle of the telephone shook me out of my peaceful concentration. Rising from my chair, I marched over to thing and barked into it: 'Yes, hello.'

It was Harry. 'Amelia, Mrs. Ramsay's gone.'

'Gone? Where?'

'I don't know. I tried to ring her up at the number she gave me, and ask her to come down to the shop, but she wasn't there. Instead I got some girl told me Mrs. Ramsay's went away somewhere, but she don't know where.'

The daughter, Mary, no doubt.

'Why would she leave like that without telling anyone?'

'I'm thinkin', maybe she didn't,' Harry said, grimly.

'What on earth do you mean?'

'Well, this girl starts askin' me who I am, and what I wanted with Mrs. Ramsay, and when I identifies myself — at least who I'm pretendin' to be — she gets all a'dither, and starts askin' things like whether I have the riddle on me, and where the shop is. Then she says I had no right to take that piece o' parchment from the family, like I'd stolen the bloomin' thing!'

'I don't like the way this is sounding, Harry. Why don't you come over here, just in case the girls raises some kind of trouble at the shop?'

'Right, ducks, I'll be over in two shakes.'

Once again, the line went dead.

At that moment, Missy came into the room, and only when I saw that she was dressed in her personal clothes did I remember that I had promised her the evening off, with the suggestion that she attend a new play at a theatre in Leicester Square. I knew, of course, that she would instead end up at the music hall, but it mattered little. She was a devoted worker and deserved a night out, even if her taste in entertainment ran the gamut from low to positively philistine. Such, I fear, is the mark of today's youth.

'Do you need anything before I go, ma'am?' she asked, clearly eager to be on her way.

'No, dear. Enjoy yourself, but do not stay out too late.'

'Right, ma'am,' she said, breezing through the door.

I began collecting up my notes and put them, along with the vellum page, into a neat stack on the day room table. It was then, amidst the complete quiet that had descended upon the house that the flaw in my reasoning regarding the riddle's solution, which had been dancing elusively at the edges of my mind, taunting me, came into clear focus. My identification of the Duke of Monmouth as 'the young Protestor,' combined with the chance discovery that the present-day Monmouth Street was once named St. Andrew's Street, were the keys that had unlocked the riddle — but how was the writer of the riddle able to look two centuries into the future and know that St. Andrew's Street was going to be renamed for the duke?

Was it merely coincidence? Divine revelation? Was the writer of the riddle some kind of seer, a Restoration version of Nostradamus? Or was the riddle itself a clever modern forgery? For all I knew of the process of dating paper and ink, the lines could have been penned a fortnight ago, drawn from an ancient legend. But a forgery to what end? It appeared that the riddle of Seven Dials had not yet given up all of its secrets.

I stepped to the window. The sky was beginning to darken. Harry should be here soon, I thought. But an hour passed and I was still awaiting his arrival. Where on earth was he? After another anxious hour, my state of nervousness and impatience had become so great that I nearly jumped bodily out of my chair when the sharp knocking came to the door. Finally, Harry had arrived. 'Missy, the door,' I called, and then remembered that she had gone. Stepping to the front door, I swung it open, only to find that it was not my diminutive friend standing there, but rather a tall, distinguished looking man of indeterminate middle age.

'I'm from Chippenham's, madam,' he said. 'The coach is waiting out front.' It was not the same driver who had come previously.

'Really? I take it, then, that Mrs. Ramsay arrived at the shop.'

'Yes, madam, she is there now. I will take you there.'

'Let me get a wrap first,' I said, leaving the man at the door while I went back inside.

'And madam, I'm to make sure that you do not forget to bring the riddle with you,' he called.

'Thank you,' I called back, throwing on a jacket. Then, after stopping to pick up the stack of papers from the table, I headed back to the door. Once outside the man led me to a common hansom cab. 'What happened to the Phaeton?' I asked.

'In use, madam. Mr. Benbow arranged for this one.'

'I see,' I muttered, starting toward the cab. Then stopped suddenly, feeling a chill inside me. 'Mr. Benbow arranged for this, you say?' I asked.

'Yes, ma'am. Is there a problem?

Indeed there was. I spun around and started back for the front door. 'I think I shall go back and telephone Chippenham's to let them know I am on my way,' I told the man.

'I think not,' the man said, rushing to

head me off. From his pocket he withdrew a small silver pistol.

'Who are you?' I demanded, striving for a defiant tone that was not supported by my emotions. 'You are not from Chippenham's.' Had the man in reality been an employee of the company, he would have referred to Harry as Mr. *Beaumont*, not Mr. *Benbow*.

'Your questions will be answered in due course,' the man said. 'For now, get in the cab.'

'I could scream, you know.'

'And I could shoot.'

Deciding that reasoning with the brute was out of the question, as was any attempt at escaping, I had no choice but to do as he said. Stepping into the cab, I sat stiffly against the seat, feeling the barrel of his gun pressed into my side. He knocked on the roof of the cab and it lurched into action.

'Give me the riddle, if you please,' he said, holding out his free hand, into which I placed the papers, including the vellum. He quickly shoved them into his coat pocket.

'Where are you taking me?' I asked.

'To my castle,' he replied.

'Your castle?'

'Every man's home is his castle, don't you agree?'

It struck me then. 'You are Charles Ramsay.'

The man nodded in agreement.

'Where is your wife?'

'That stupid creature I honoured with my family name?' he spat, his voice rising dangerously. 'You will not be hearing from her again.'

'What have you done with her?' I asked, feeling chilled by more than the night air.

'She betrayed me, Mrs. Watson, and I am not a man with a stomach for betrayal. No doubt she sobbed on your shoulder about me, told you that I was some kind of cold and heartless beast. I have reasons for my actions, just as I have certain established certain rules governing my home. The most important rule is that what is mine is not to be placed in the hands of others. That applies nowhere more strongly than to that piece of parchment she took from me and gave to you. Jane committed the unpardonable; she removed the riddle from the house without my knowledge and shared its information with others.'

'She only wanted to make you happy,' I said.

'I did not wed her for happiness, but for what she could give me. The common little fool never realized that.'

I faced straight ahead as we careened through the narrow streets toward our destination. 'What is going to happen to me?' I asked, my fear tempered with indignation.

'You possess knowledge that I require,' he said. 'After I have obtained that knowledge, you will have fulfilled your usefulness to me and will be discarded.'

'*Discarded?*' I cried, indignantly.

He pushed the pistol deeper into my side. 'Careful, madam. You would be wrong to assume that I will not shoot you if I have to, whether I have retrieved your information or not. Mr. Benbow has told me enough about the solution to the riddle to convince me that I could piece together the rest myself.'

'Where is Harry?'

'He is safe. For the time being.'

I glanced up at the ceiling, but the wretch beside me seemed to read my very thoughts. 'Do not waste your time wondering if you could alert the driver,' he said. 'I have taken the liberty of telling him that you were mentally unstable. He has been instructed — and paid — to ignore whatever he might hear emanating from inside the cab.'

We drove on in nerve-wracking silence for another three-quarters of an hour, and then the cab began to slow.

'Here we are,' Ramsay said. 'I appreciate the fact that you did not try to do anything foolish. A woman with common sense is a rare thing these days, Mrs. Watson, and I congratulate you.'

'You may keep your congratulations to yourself!' I bristled.

My rising anger made Ramsay smile. Or perhaps it was my rising helplessness. 'Now then,' he said, 'I will get out first, keeping the pistol trained on you, and then you will emerge slowly and walk beside me, straight to the door.'

I remained silent as he stepped out of the cab and, hiding the pistol from the driver, paid for the ride. Then following his demands, I slowly stepped down and remained at his side. Together, we watched the cab disappear down the dark street, which was empty, except for the presence another hansom that was stopped at the curb several houses down. I knew that any attempt to race down the street and alert the driver of that cab would meet with disaster.

Ramsay's 'castle' turned out to be a modest, brick dwelling in Lambeth, into which he ushered me. As soon as we were inside the house, I heard Harry's voice calling: 'Amelia, are you all right?'

Another voice bellowed, 'Shut up, you!' That was followed by the sound of a hard slap.

'Harry!' I shouted.

'He is in there,' Ramsay said, nudging me with the pistol. 'Go on.'

I stepped into a comfortably furnished, though dimly lit, room. Harry Benbow was tied to a chair, his hair plastered against his forehead with perspiration. Standing over him was a young girl whose face bore a scowling expression, and who was looking at me with the most lifeless eyes I had ever seen.

'I'm sorry, Amelia,' Harry moaned. 'They forced me to tell 'em where to find you. I'm sorry for everything, ducks.'

I directed my gaze back upon the girl. 'You are Mary Ramsay, I presume.' The girl sneered.

'Mary, show some manners,' Ramsay commanded, prompting her to perform a parody of a smile, one that revealed large, crooked teeth. 'How d'you do?' she growled.

Ramsay pulled a chair to the center of the room and pushed me into it, and instructed the girl to tie me up as she had Harry. All the while he kept the pistol trained on me. Mary Ramsay carried out her task with deliberate roughness, and the ropes painfully chafed my wrists. 'Must they be so tight?' I groaned to Ramsay.

'They must,' he replied. 'I am a not a man who can afford to take chances.'

'You are not a man at all, you are *swine*,' I riposted, but then cried out as the girl grabbed a handful of my hair and yanked it, wrenching my head backwards.

'I don't think you know who you're talking to,' she said. 'You should be down on the floor, scraping before your sovereign, the rightful King of England!'

Thankfully, she let go of my hair, and I rested my pained gaze upon Ramsay again. 'You are the rightful King of England?'

He bowed. 'As was my father, and his father, and every male member of my family since the time of William of Orange, the usurper who turned the country inexorably away from the True Church.' He paced before me, taking slow, measured steps. 'I am a direct lineal descendant of James the second, the last Catholic King of the realm, and the last true monarch. Even though my family name is not to be found on any accepted genealogical chart, my descent from James is a fact.'

'In other words, your ancestor was illegitimate,' I said.

'I could tell right off he was a bastard,' Harry added, then with an abashed glance to me, added: 'Pardon my tongue, Amelia.'

Poor Harry's misplaced concern with propriety in the face of such grave danger drew from me a helpless, mirthless chuckle. Unfortunately, the wretched girl behind me mistook my laughter as a comment on her father's statement, and grabbed my hair once more, giving my head a vicious twist.

'Mary!' Ramsay shouted. 'How many times must I tell you: *noblesse oblige*.' The girl let go.

I shook my aching head. 'What do you want from me, *your majesty*?' I invested as much venom as possible into the last two words. If Ramsay took offense, he did not show it.

'The final answer to the riddle,' he replied. 'The exact location of the treasure.'

'Why are you so certain there is a treasure?' I asked.

'Oh, it is there, Mrs. Watson. That which the riddle terms a 'relick' is actually the remainder of the fortune in gold and jewels that was raised to finance the Monmouth rebellion. When the unfortunate duke lost his bid to become king — and his head as well — what was left of his war chest was secreted, with the knowledge that one day, the rightful monarch, the one destined by God to rule this empire, would rise up and retake the throne from the bloodline of pretenders. I am ready to fulfill that destiny, and the destiny of the True Church. That treasure will finance this ascension.'

He stopped and smiled.

'Ironic, is it not? That the wealth that was gathered by a Protestant in an attempt to overthrow the last Catholic king will now be used to restore the status of the Catholic Church in the empire?'

'Insane would be my description,' I replied. 'You cannot seriously believe that you will be crowned.'

'Me? Alas, no. Perhaps if one of my forebears had seen fit to accept his God-bestowed destiny, I might have been, but I have resigned myself to the likelihood that I will never sit on the throne of England. It is not for myself that I do this,

Mrs. Watson, but rather for my son. Properly used and invested, the treasure could reap wealth beyond even my dreams, and with wealth comes power. Imagine, a male of royal blood being born into that kind of wealth and power. What could not that blessed boy accomplish?'

Suddenly I realized how this mad plot was hinged. 'It is not simply the treasure that you are lacking, is it?' I said. 'You do not have a son either, do you, Mr. Ramsay? That is the reason you married such a young woman, so you could breed a male heir. That was the thing she could give you.'

'And it is the reason I will marry another young woman, and another after her, and another after her, if that is what it takes,' Ramsay declared. 'I *will* have a son! I will not suffer the fates of James and the heretic Henry, with only daughters to carry on after me.'

He cast a contemptuous glance at Mary.

'And if they do not produce a son, you will kill them so you can marry again.'

'What are a few individual lives

compared to the restoration of the True Church?' he shouted. 'The lives of those women mean nothing.'

'How *dare* you purport to be a man of faith?' I spat. 'You are sickening, a disgrace —'

'That is enough!' he thundered, quieting me. 'I have no interest in wasting more any time on a debate whose outcome has already been decided. You have been very clever in solving the riddle, Mrs. Watson, I will give you that. While I am certain that I would have eventually been able to decipher it myself, you have saved me valuable time, and I am not ungrateful. But now I need the last piece of the puzzle.' He knelt down before me, pushing his face close to mine, placing the barrel of the pistol against my heart. 'Where is the treasure buried?'

'I . . . do not . . . know,' I stammered, struggling to overcome my revulsion and fear.

'Leave her be!' Harry cried out, prompting Mary to rushed over to his chair and viciously cuff him across the face.

'I do not know!' I shouted. 'The

solution to the riddle is Seven Dials, and I believe that at a certain time of day the column of Seven Dials cast a shadow over the hiding place of the treasure, but what time, I do not know!'

Ramsay rose to his feet and backed away, and I was relieved to be spared the unpleasant heat of his breath. 'I believe you, Mrs. Watson. You have convinced me that neither you nor Benbow have the information I seek. For me, that is a small setback. It does, however, mean that the two of you are no longer needed.'

He spun around to Harry and leveled the pistol at his chest. Harry's eyes widened and he struggled helplessly against his bounds. I turned my head away and closed my eyes. I could not watch. I waited for the dreadful sound of the bullet.

But instead of the shot, I heard another sound: a loud pounding on the door of the house. I opened my eyes to see Ramsay glance toward his daughter, who had started toward the door. 'Ignore it, ignore it!' he demanded, raising the gun again. But the pounding continued, only now it came from two different directions.

'They're at the back, too!' Mary cried.

I heard a muffled cry that very nearly reduced me to tears of joy: '*Police, open up!*'

'*Gor*, the peelers!' Harry cried, jubilantly.

I dared not to even wonder why the police had chosen this particular time to descend upon the Ramsay house, for fear they might go away again!

Clearly as confused and frightened as they were angered by the development, Ramsay and Mary looked at each other, as though uncertain as to what to do next. A moment later we heard the splintering sound of a door being burst open, and a second after that, a half-dozen uniformed PC's entered the room, batons poised.

In front of the brigade was a sergeant who trained his pistol on the stunned Ramsay and easily disarmed him.

Mary was not so acquiescent. Fighting like a madwoman, it required the combined force of three constables to hold her. Despite everything, I could not bring myself to hate the wretched girl. She was a creature of her demented father's making, and as such, probably never had a chance.

Another officer was working to untie Harry and me. My arms, when released, felt like molten lead. A bruise was forming on Harry's cheek, where Mary had struck him. When the situation was under control, the sergeant turned to me. 'You must be Mrs. Watson,' he said.

'Yes, but how on earth . . . how . . . ?' For one of the few times in my life, I was speechless.

'Come along outside, madam. You too, sir.' He beckoned to Harry.

As the constables were escorting both Ramsays to a police wagon, I overheard Charles Ramsay ranting to no one in particular: 'This is not the end! I will have a son! If he be born in prison, so be it!' I shook my head, feeling an uneasy mix of pity and revulsion.

I was still puzzling over the perfectly-timed arrival of the police when I looked up and saw something even more puzzling: there, before me, stood Sherlock Holmes! He trod over to where I was standing, the expression on his face a conflicting mixture of concern and something resembling embarrassment. For a brief moment, I thought he was going to reach out and lay a comforting hand on my arm, but if that was his inclination, he fought it. 'I trust you are unharmed, Mrs. Watson?' he said, awkwardly.

'Barely,' I gasped, feeling weak. 'And I must assume that you are the means of my escape from the hands of a madman, but how on earth did you know where to find me? How did you even know I was in trouble?'

'I happened to arrive in front of your home in time to witness you being threatened by the man who was just placed into custody,' he answered. 'I could tell immediately that something was amiss by the tension and rigidity in your body. What's more, the man was standing far too close to you for this to be an innocent conversation. I secreted myself in the shadows and watched until I discerned a glint of metal from the man's hand, which I immediately recognized as the barrel of a pistol. After you were forced into the cab, I hailed one of my own and instructed the driver to follow you, which we did the entire way here.'

'Then that was your cab I saw at the end of the street,' I said.

'Yes. Once more I watched as you were forced to enter the house, and no sooner were you inside than I sent the driver to fetch the police while keeping watch outside. The constables quickly arrived, and the rest you know.'

'Oh, heaven help me,' I moaned, now fearing I might collapse. The only thing that kept me upright was my refusal to faint away in a womanish swoon in front of Mr. Holmes.

'Perhaps heaven already has,' he uttered. 'While I am not a fervent believer in the hand of Providence interfering with the affairs of mortals, I have to question whether the influence of a mightier force was not involved in placing me at the right place at exactly the right time to facilitate your delivery.'

'Mr. Holmes, don't tell me you believe you were directed to Queen Anne Street by the will of God!' I said, startled by the the admission.

'It is only the timing that gives me pause for thought,' the detective replied. Then, lowering his voice, so that none of the constables hovering about the scene would be able to hear, he said: 'The reason for coming to your home was far more commonplace: I came to return your dress.'

I stared at him for a moment, and then burst out in loud, nearly hysterical laughter. 'Mr. Holmes,' I gasped, 'you may keep the dress.'

He regarded me with a startled expression, and then likewise broke into an explosive laugh. It was the first time I had ever seen such a sign of mirth coming from Sherlock Holmes.

A moment later, he regained control of himself. 'I have no wish to detain you further, Mrs. Watson,' he said, a sardonic smile curling his thin lips. 'That is the job of the police. Good evening.'

With that, he turned around, strode almost invisibly through the crowd that had started to collect on the street, and disappeared into the night. The next thing I knew, Harry, who had finished regaling the police with the story of his abduction, came to my side.

'*Gor*, ducks,' he said, looking into the milling crowd, 'was that *him* you was talkin' to?'

I nodded. 'That was Sherlock Holmes.'

'So you found out a way to contact him?'

'Yes, from now on I shall leave a note for him at my cleaners,' I said, and then I began to giggle helplessly again, much to the puzzlement of my old friend.

After being fully questioned by the police, I was finally allowed to go home.

It was nearly midnight by the time I returned to Queen Anne Street, where I was welcomed with open arms by Missy, who had come home early from the music hall, found the house empty, and spent the last two hours working herself nearly to distraction over my unexplained absence.

After offering slightly more assurance than I actually felt that I was fine, I retired to my bed, where I slept well into the next morning.

Not surprisingly, Harry turned up at our door that day. The fancy dress suit was now gone, and instead he wore his more familiar threadbare brown jacket and battered bowler hat.

I expected him to report that he had been let go by the firm of Chippenham and Co., which by now must have learned the details of his deception, but instead he told me that he had resigned.

'Hobnobbin' with them upper-class toffs'll land you in trouble every time,' he said, with a grin.

The story of the Ramsays received little press coverage until the body of Jane Ramsay was uncovered inside their Lambeth home, two days later. After that, the story was on the front page of every newspaper — the headline in the *Illustrated London News* read, *The Man Who Would Be King*, with no apologies whatsoever to Mr. Kipling — and reporters began collecting and swarming in front of our home. Despite my best attempts to minimize it, they naturally played to the hilt my association with my ultimate savior, Sherlock Holmes.

Reporters will write what they will write, of course, though I cannot say that

Harry was much help to my cause. Reveling in the spotlight, like any good actor, he took every opportunity to publicly characterize me as the natural successor to Mr. Holmes, whom, he was quick to point out, became involved in the case only after I had done the crucial work involved in solving the puzzle.

What Mr. Holmes thought of all this I have no idea.

Within a week, the furor had died down sufficiently to allow Missy and me to go about our normal routines without being accosted by packs of men carrying notebooks and pens. But I could not divest myself of the memory of Mr. Holmes's words. Had, indeed, Providence become involved? Had it somehow chosen the exact moment for Sherlock Holmes to come to our home, knowing that either a minute earlier or later would have meant that both Harry and I would now be lying in hidden graves? Were we, as human beings, engaged in some kind of grand design that was beyond our comprehension?

Or was Mr. Holmes's sudden arrival merely a fortunate happenstance of chance?

Were we, after all, simply slaves to the random acts of every other human being? How different would all of history, indeed, all of civilization, be if any one of the million tiny, individual acts and decisions that are carried out each day, had been carried out differently? It was staggering to contemplate.

I was not able to push the riddle of the young Protestor out of my mind until John's arrival back from his lecture tour (and while I still intended to take up the matter of his providing Mr. Holmes with a key to our home with him, it somehow seemed less imperative to do so at once). I had striven to completely banish it from my thoughts, and for the most part had succeeded. Or so I believed.

It was not until some two months after the events had transpired, when the pleasant crispness of autumn had given way to the grey wetness of winter, that I suddenly lurched up in bed, having been thrust out of a particularly vivid dream in which I was once more studying the vellum page containing the riddle.

The document in my dream was

identical to the real thing, except that the phrase *St. Andrews cross* had been set apart in vibrant golden letters.

'St. Andrew's cross,' I uttered aloud in bed, hoping that my sudden rising did not awaken John.

Unlike the Calvary cross, St. Andrew's cross was in the shape of an X. Or, in Roman numerals — which was the style of number most likely to be found on a sundial — *ten*.

'The time at which the relick may be founde.'

It had to be the missing piece of the puzzle. When the sun struck the column precisely at ten o'clock in the morning — ten in the evening not having sufficient sunlight, even in midsummer — its shadow would point like a finger directly to the 'relick's' burial location.

I must inform Harry of this!

But in the next instant, another vivid image appeared in my mind. I saw Harry dressed as a pirate, toting a shovel in one hand and a pickaxe in the other. '*X marks the spot, my girl,*' I could hear him saying. '*And who knows what kind of bloodthirsty excitement we'll find this time around?'*

I laughed and shuddered at the same time.

John moaned and rolled over, but did not awaken.

'I'm sorry, Harry,' I whispered, 'but this secret will remain with me.'

With that, I settled down and drifted back to sleep.

We do hope that you have enjoyed reading this large print book.

Did you know that all of our titles are available for purchase?

We publish a wide range of high quality large print books including:

Romances, Mysteries, Classics
General Fiction
Non Fiction and Westerns

Special interest titles available in large print are:

The Little Oxford Dictionary
Music Book, Song Book
Hymn Book, Service Book

Also available from us courtesy of Oxford University Press:

Young Readers' Dictionary
(large print edition)
Young Readers' Thesaurus
(large print edition)

For further information or a free brochure, please contact us at:
Ulverscroft Large Print Books Ltd.,
The Green, Bradgate Road, Anstey,
Leicester, LE7 7FU, England.
Tel: (00 44) **0116 236 4325**
Fax: (00 44) **0116 234 0205**

Other titles in the
Linford Mystery Library:

MISSION: TANK WAR

Michael Kurland

1960s: A small, oil-rich Arab nation is about to lose its status as a protectorate of Britain, and waiting in the wings to invade is a superior enemy force led by Soviet tanks. On a mission to stop them is debonair agent Peter Carthage and the men from War (Weapons Analysis and Research), Inc., a company with an ultra-scientific approach to warfare. How many men from War, Inc. does it take to stop an army of tanks? Six — plus one beautiful, plucky young British woman determined to rescue a kidnapped brother.

GIVE THE GIRL A GUN

Richard Deming

Manville Moon is a private investigator. On a night out with his girlfriend Fausta Moreni, the lovely owner of the El Patio Café, a group of customers invites them both to a private party at an inventor's home, to celebrate the launch of a business venture based on his new device. But soon after their arrival, the inventor is shot dead by an unseen assailant. Police suspicion quickly falls on the boyfriend of one of the guests, and Moon is hired to prove his innocence — plunging him and Fausta into deadly danger . . .

DEATH ON THE TURNING TIDE

Katherine Hutton

Nick Shaw jumps at the chance to explore the island of Jersey for his job as a travel writer. Accompanying him is his journalist friend Ben Ryland, who wants to follow up a story about modern-day smuggling that could be his big break. Disregarding the risks, Ryland hares off to probe further into a suspicious death — only to vanish without a trace. Searching for him, Shaw is inexorably drawn into the world of smuggling — where the wrong move can lead to a watery grave . . .